Wakefield Press

GUS AND THE
BURNING STONES

Troy Hunter is an adult and YA author whose short stories have appeared in a variety of publications and journals. He lives in Melbourne and works as a marketing and communications consultant.

His first Gus novel, *Gus and the Missing Boy*, came out in 2024 and was shortlisted for the 2024 Ned Kelly Awards – Best Debut Crime Fiction, and the BAD Sydney Crime Writers Festival 2025 Danger Awards.

He is also the co-host of the Queer Writes Sessions podcast.

troyhunterwriter.com

Praise for *Gus and the Burning Stones*

'*Gus and the Burning Stones* is a ripper of a novel. A real page-turner with all the twists and turns you expect from a gripping mystery, combined with the angst of young people trying to find themselves. Troy Hunter's prose is witty, sharp and energetic – and, most importantly, brimming with compassion for his teenage characters in their vulnerable moments.'

—**Holden Sheppard**, award-winning author of *King of Dirt* (2025), *The Brink* (2022), and *Invisible Boys* (2019)

'Gus, Shell and Kane are back with another twisty whodunnit adventure. *Gus and the Burning Stones* has multiple mysteries, secrets and lies, all wrapped up in a great story that will keep you guessing to the very end. If you blended Agatha Christie with a loveable Aussie teen, you'd end up with Gus!'

—**Amy Doak**, award-winning author of the *Eleanor Jones* series

'Where there's smoke, there's murder – Gus, Shell and Kane are back, funny and fearless as ever, in a mystery that'll keep you gripped till the end. Chasing a lead on his birth mum, Gus finds himself trapped in a storm with a dead body and a community of off-grid weirdos who can't or won't tell the truth.'

—**R.W.R. McDonald**, award-winning author of *An Ambush of Widows* (2024) and *The Nancys* series

'I loved *Gus and the Burning Stones*: a mystery romp with a twisty plot, characters I cared desperately about and a huge beating heart at its centre.'

—**Kate Emery**, award-winning author of *My Family and Other Suspects* (2024) and *The Not So Chosen One* (2022)

GUS AND THE BURNING STONES

TROY HUNTER

Wakefield
Press

Wakefield Press
16 Rose Street
Mile End
South Australia 5031
www.wakefieldpress.com.au

First published 2025

Supported by a grant from the Government of South Australia.

Cover designed by Josh Durham, Design by Committee
Text designed by Jesse Pollard, Wakefield Press
Edited by Maddy Sexton, Wakefield Press
Typeset by Greenhill Publishing

ISBN 978 1 92338 800 0

A catalogue record for this
book is available from the
National Library of Australia

Dedicated to Dean Walliss and Bianca Rogers

Contents

This book discusses some serious issues including anxiety, self-harm, and death by burning.
Mentions of self-harm appear on pages
4, 36, 42, 65, 67, 68, 69, 122, 132 and 210.

This book was written on the unceded lands of the Wurundjeri people of the Kulin Nation. The author acknowledges the Traditional Owners and custodians of the lands on which he works, and pays his respect to Elders past and present, as well as to any Indigenous Australians reading this book.

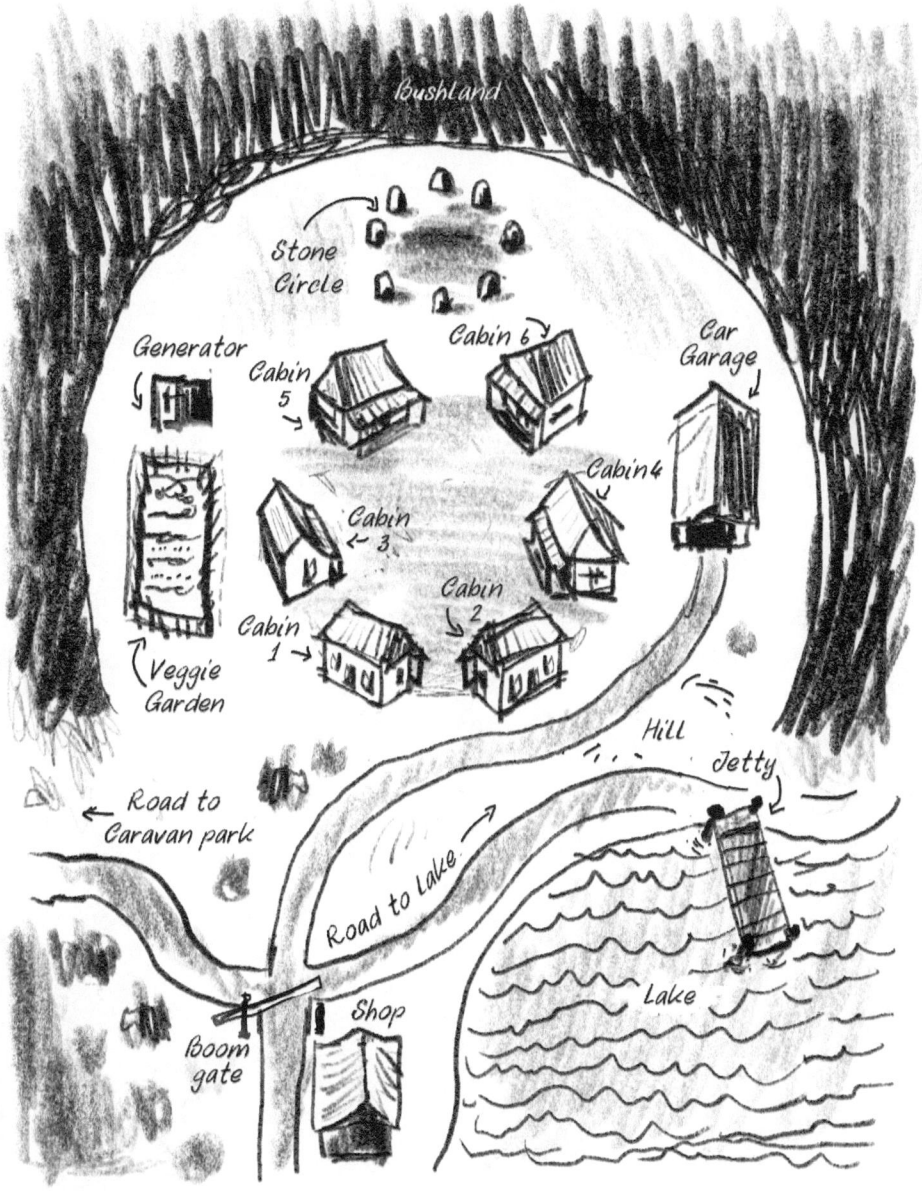

Prologue

We're all standing in the middle of the lounge, reeling from what we've just discovered. The murder, the stone circle, my mother . . . I've figured it out. It's all connected.

We don't have time to process any of this though, because the cabin is on fire around us. The side wall is warping and buckling in the heat, and the room is filling with smoke.

Through the window, I can just make out a figure standing outside. They're wearing a black hoodie that hides their face, like a character in a horror film.

They're watching, waiting.

We rush to the front door, but it's stuck. My eyes and throat are burning from the smoke. Kane picks up a chair from the kitchen and throws it through the glass of the front door. The sudden rush of cool air from outside is a relief, but it makes the flames whoosh with intensity. Picking up one of the broken chair legs, Kane smashes the remaining glass away from the frame.

Before I have time to react, Shell grabs some towels and runs them under the cold tap.

'Take these!' she yells, flinging a towel to me and Kane. I wrap it around my head and shoulders, like she is doing. 'Now run!' she gasps, pushing me and Kane toward the door.

We stumble out of the cabin and start sprinting. Taking a backwards glance at the flames, I spot Hoodie coming toward us.

'They're coming!' I yell. We're all panting with the effort as we push faster.

'Help! Fire!' Shell yells as she runs. Where is everyone?

I'm looking around wildly in desperation when a glow further up the hill catches my eye. The stone circle is on fire too! What the hell is going on? How can stones burn?

Everyone is outrunning me. Hoodie is gaining on me. I'm too fat and slow to outrun them. I feel faint, like the world is swirling around me, taking me away. The ground disappears and I fall. When I scramble back up it's too late. I'm caught.

Suddenly Hoodie is right here. They lean over me and pull back their hood. 'Gus.'

'You?' I say in shock.

Chapter 1

Toastie

I'm walking along the main corridor at school, idly running my library card in my hand along the locker doors, enjoying the clacking noise on the metal, as I head toward my detective agency. It sounds good to say that . . . *my detective agency.*

Hazleton High is a nondescript series of white buildings set among the old Victorian houses and small apartments of Hazleton, Melbourne. It's not the best or the worst school, just another underfunded public school. Still, it has a good library, which is where I spend half my time anyway.

The detective agency started as an assignment for Business Studies last year. Miss Wright, the school principal, actually indulged Shell and me and let us set it up for real after we managed to solve a cold crime case with our friend Kane. I think she agreed to it because she assumed there'd be no cases. She was right. Not even a missing laptop or a stolen lunch.

The agency is a tiny old stationery storage room. All that fits inside is a tiny desk, some shelves, and two chairs. But it has a cool split door so that the top opens while the bottom stays shut, like a tuckshop. Shell and I keep the top open when we're in there. We're both fat, so it's a miracle we both fit at the same time.

Shell Oliver, my best mate and co-detective, is already here, eating a toastie with her headphones on. She's probably listening to a true crime podcast, as always.

Her dark hair is clipped back so short that it's virtually shaved now. She's wearing no make-up but still her big, vivid dark eyes twinkle brightly with a combination of brains and kindness. She's dressed in all black as usual, wearing a round badge that says, 'Fight climate change – there's no place like home'.

'Any cases come in today?' A detective asked his secretary this in an old noir film I watched once, but it doesn't sound as cool in real life.

She looks up, clearly a little startled that I've appeared, then takes her headphones off, smiling up at me.

'No,' she laughs. 'We may need to steal something ourselves just to drum up business.'

'Anything to get out of this storage room, hey?'

After the way our detective careers started, it's no wonder we're bored. Solving a cold case that we found on a missing kids website would have been impressive enough, but we also discovered that my parents weren't my biological family.

Anyway, it was a literal adventure, with a road trip, suspects, investigating the case with a retired detective . . . but I never did find out what happened to my birth mother, Jane. She disappeared off the radar years ago.

Solving the case totally turned my life upside down. My whole identity felt like it was in flux, blurring before me, splintering through time. My mental health was all over the place and I was having panic attacks and self-harming. I couldn't have gotten through it without Shell and Kane supporting me and saving me, literally. I still see a psych every week, Dr Yamada, but I feel like I'm starting to put the past behind me.

One thing that hasn't changed is I still want to join the police as soon as I'm old enough.

'Check it,' I say. Out of my backpack I produce a loosely rolled-up piece of A3 card. It's white with the words 'Hazleton High Detective Agency' printed in bold lettering.

She smiles at it wryly, takes it and holds it up in front of her. 'Nice. Pointless, but nice.'

'I've got some double-sided tape to put it on the door,' I add. She nods half-heartedly.

'What's wrong? You look like crap,' I say.

'Wow, rude,' she snorts.

'It's not just the no make-up thing. Which, by the way, I think is a misstep for you.'

She rolls her eyes. 'Your opinion is noted and filed under "piss off".'

Grinning, I get the tape out and lay the sign on the floor. It won't flatten properly so I've got one hand on one corner, a knee on another, my bag on a third, like a sad game of Twister.

'Seriously though, are you okay?' I ask, taping one corner then another while trying and failing to stop it rolling back into itself.

'Things have been weird with Mum and Dad. They want to up my sessions with my psych and they keep asking me cringe questions.'

'About being non-binary?'

'Yeah. It's like I've told them I'm vegetarian, but they think I could change my mind at any moment and start inhaling bacon.'

'Yikes.'

'I brought up gender neutral pronouns the other day, and they got very confused. I didn't get any further than that.'

'I'm sure they'll get used to it in time.' As usual, I don't know what to say to Shell. I try to put on a sympathetic face, but I feel so useless. I open my laptop as a distraction.

Shell knows me well and changes the subject. 'Did Kane get that job?'

I shake my head. 'He didn't even get an interview.' Kane is my other best friend, and my next-door neighbour. He's only nineteen but he's basically like an older brother to me. He hasn't been able to find a job since he dropped out of high school two years ago.

Shell's eyebrows climb high. 'If a meathead like him can't get a basic job in a gym, then what hope is there?'

Shell and Kane have a . . . tenuous relationship. She's right though. Working in a gym seemed like the ideal gig for him. They told him he has no experience and no qualifications, despite the fact that he lives for lifting weights and footy, so he's actually perfect for the job.

'I told him to look into TAFE courses, but he—'

I've been talking while checking my emails and messages. There's a new message from the website that kicked off the cold case investigation last year.

'What is it?' asks Shell.

I look up at her, unable to speak.

'What?' she asks again, more urgently.

I don't know what to say so I spin the laptop toward her and point.

IF YOU WANT TO FIND YOUR BIRTH MOTHER, COME TO THE CIRCLE.

Shell peers at the screen, her eyes widening as she reads.

'What the hell! What is "The Circle"?'

'No clue. Whoever sent this added a link to Google Maps, so it must be a place.'

'Any idea who it's from?'

I shake my head, clicking my mouse around the message. 'It doesn't say. It looks like it's from an anonymous server.'

The last time I investigated a case we found on this website, it changed my entire life. Now someone is using the same site to tell me I can find Jane? It seems too good to be true.

Hoping it's not some phishing scam, I click on the link. At first nothing happens. Then Google Maps opens up to a campsite near Lake Walliss. Only three-ish hours' drive from Melbourne.

'It sounds like a cult,' says Shell.

'I know, right?' I shudder. This is so weird.

'Wait, screenshot the message, in case it disappears!' yelps Shell.

Good idea. I scramble to screenshot it, heart pounding.

'Are you going to respond?' she asks.

What do I say? How do you adequately respond to something like this? *Okay, sure. Leaving now!*

'Here goes nothing,' I say, typing a message and hitting send before I have time to change my mind: *Is this Jane?*

Shell and I hold our breaths.

There's no response. We are both staring intensely at the screen for like a minute, waiting for something to happen. The school period buzzer goes off and we both jump out of our skins.

The spell broken, we pack up our stuff and squeeze our way out of the cupboard.

'Text me if you get an answer,' calls Shell as she disappears down the hall toward her Economics class. Despite her size she walks with poise and dignity. Unlike me, who lurches from place to place.

My next class is Modern History, but I find myself standing in the hallway, frozen in time. All I can think of is my own history and how I have so many lingering questions that are still unanswered. There are huge chunks of myself that are still a mystery to me. If I go to this Circle, will I actually get to meet my birth mother for the first time? Will some of these questions finally be answered? What if it turns out to be some kind of prank?

After all the drama of last year, I feel panicky about meeting her. What if she doesn't like me? What if I don't like her? Where has she been all these years? Why hasn't she found me before now? Did she even look? And what about Meg, my adoptive mum – how will she feel if I find Jane?

So many questions. There are too many tabs open in my brain right now.

Chapter 2

Knitting

Walking my bike home after school along the railway tracks, my head is buzzing with questions. There's still no response to my message.

I wheel my bike through the carport and into the backyard, parking it near the patch of soil where my childhood cubbyhouse used to stand. I smashed it all up last year, as part of processing what had happened to me. There were too many bad memories trapped inside its walls.

Mum's asleep in her room, so I head to the spotless kitchen, grab some leftovers, and flop on the couch with the container sitting on my chest.

As I eat, I overthink the message and what it could mean. Could Jane have sent it? Could it be someone else entirely that I don't even know, but knows her, or knows my story? There was heaps of media coverage when we solved the case and everything became public last year, so it could be anyone really.

If Jane is still out there, why hasn't she been in touch? Every day since it hit the mainstream news, I've been hoping I'd get a message from her. Something to say that she's been looking for me all these years and now she's finally found me and she wants to meet and start making up for lost time. Not much to ask.

But that message never came. Its absence is like a hole inside me.

I google 'The Circle' but nothing useful comes up, just random results from TV shows to geometry to abstract art. Even adding the location near Lake Walliss generates nothing.

I hear a noise from down the hall and realise Mum must have woken up. I get up and head down the hall to her room. You can tell it's an unwell person's space. The blinds are down, there are medicine bottles on her bedside table, and bandages and surgical stockings are strewn on the chair in one corner.

She's a tiny shape in the huge bed.

I pull up the blinds and let the afternoon sun in.

'Gussy, you look like a worried beagle. What's going on? Something happen at school?'

I take in her drawn face and slight frame. Her short hair is greyer than last year, matching the greyness of her skin. She's in a lot of pain and on strong medication for her legs, which were crushed in a car accident a few years ago, but it still shocks me sometimes how sick she looks. It also spooks me that she can read me like a book, even if she does compare me to weird animals sometimes.

'Tell me what's wrong,' she says, hoisting herself up into a sitting position against her variety of pillows.

I show her the message. She reads it carefully.

'That bloody website,' she frowns. 'Frankly, it causes nothing but trouble. Why are you still looking at it?'

'I thought Jane might message me there and try to get in touch,' I mumble. I try not to talk about my birth mother around her too much, but I only found out about her last year, so it's hard not to. I don't want to rub it in that Mum – Meg – isn't my biological mother, but I also can't ignore that Jane exists. At the end of the day, Meg is my real mum in all the ways that matter.

Mum nods. 'Of course, that makes sense. I imagine that website got a lot of traffic from gawkers after your story was in the papers.'

I laugh quietly at how she refers to the media as 'the papers' – so boomer.

'Have you ever heard of this place?' I ask.

'No, but I don't like the sound of it.'

'Would you be super worried if I went there to find out?' I ask, not looking directly at her.

She leans forward and puts her hands on both sides of my square face. I can smell the bleach on her fingers from her endless cleaning. 'Not at all. You have a complete right to find out as much as possible about your past. I would never stand in the way of that, Gussy, not anymore.'

I smile at her in relief.

I love that we can talk openly about this now. Last year she was keeping secrets from me, and I was doing DNA tests behind her back and taking off interstate without telling her. Somehow going through what we did last year has rebalanced us. Obviously things aren't perfect, and she's still a parent and says and does parent-y things, but she no longer treats me like a child. I'm way more honest with her too, most of the time.

'But can you wait another week or so? My legs are giving me hell lately, so I'm not sure I could sit in a car for hours, let alone drive.'

Of course she can't drive me a few hours away right now. But I want to go now, like today. This is the closest I've gotten to finding out more about Jane and I don't want the lead to go cold.

'I'm not sure I can wait that long,' I say quietly.

She frowns, then reaches over to the bedside table for her knitting. I can see her thinking as the clacking of needles fills the silence between us.

'I don't know, Gussy,' she begins. 'I worry about you. Look what happened last time you followed a trail from that website. You ended up in real danger.'

She's right of course. I'm a trouble magnet.

'What if I went with Kane and Shell?' I ask. 'It's not that far. We could be up and back in a day or so.'

She continues knitting, taking a moment. The wool is purple and I have no idea what she's actually trying to make. All I know is it looks a bit . . . rough around the edges. Some stitches seem tighter than others and it all looks uneven, from what I can see.

As if reading my mind, Mum sighs. 'Taking up knitting instead of smoking has not been successful,' she says, holding up her work to the light. 'So many holes.' She pokes a finger though one.

'Mum, *please*. I need to know.'

She concentrates on her knitting. 'I guess your past is like this isn't it, holes where answers should be.'

'Yes.' I exhale. She gets it, I think.

Those holes are manageable some days, but other days they threaten to swallow me up like a black hole on *Doctor Who*. If I had a TARDIS then maybe I could navigate them better, but all I have is me. And unlike the TARDIS, which is bigger on the inside than the outside, I feel like I'm big on the outside but small on the inside.

She looks up at me, a mixture of sadness and understanding in her eyes. 'Let me talk to Fiona about Kane and Cheryl about Shell, then I'll get back to you.'

'Thank you, Mum. I mean it.' If Mum's okay with it, Kane and Shell's mums will be too. They worry less than she does.

As I leave the room, I hear her start humming some sad song to herself as she returns to her knitting.

Chapter 3

Sandbags

As Kane's boxy, shit-brown 1970s Kingswood turns another corner too quickly on the winding, hilly road toward Lake Walliss, my stomach lurches again. As much as I do think his car is cool, it's not built for the twisty turns in these hills. Still, it's also making the *Doctor Who* bobblehead glued to the dash bounce like crazy, which is funny.

Kane is in his happy place, hooning around in the car, wearing his wraparound sunnies. Despite the cold, he is wearing his uniform of T-shirt and shorts. I'm rugged up with a denim jacket and jeans next to him, feeling a bit anxious about what's going to happen when we get to this circle place. Shell is in the back seat, eating chips and listening to true crime podcasts, her big red headphones matching the red woollen beanie covering her head. Am I the only one who feels queasy? The harsh wind battering the car isn't helping, but there's more to it than that.

It's been nearly three hours since we left Melbourne, so we must be almost there. Even though it's only 3.15 pm, the sky is already starting to get dark. Ominous clouds are rolling in above us, fat with rain. The weather report warned that a major storm front was coming up this way. Mum wanted me to wait till next weekend, when the weather would be better, but I told her I didn't care about some storm and just wanted answers. I'm glad she's supporting me doing this, looking for Jane.

The darkening sky seems sinister somehow. I wonder if I should have listened to Mum? Feeling guilty, I try to call her, but my phone has no bars.

Kane points to the Google Maps directions on his phone. The map has frozen. 'Signal is really patchy here, but it's okay, I reckon I know where to go from here.'

I wind down the window manually and let the brutal blast of cold air smack my face.

'Oi!' snaps Shell, as her bag of chips gets blown out of her hand.

'Sorry!' I say and wind it back up as quickly as I can.

What if this is a massive waste of time? The message was so vague, and I never heard anything after I replied, so I've got no way of knowing if this is a real lead or not. But I have to try and find out. What other choice is there?

'We're nearly there, skinhead,' says Kane, grinning at Shell in the rear-view mirror. She self-consciously touches the beanie covering her head.

'Thanks, musclehead,' she replies, deadpan.

He laughs. 'Oh, you noticed? I'm getting bigger every day.' He takes one hand off the steering wheel to do a quick bicep flex.

Shell holds his gaze in the mirror. A strong, steady look. 'What are you overcompensating for with all this bodybuilding?'

Kane scowls at her, still not looking at the road. The car swerves.

'Both hands on the wheel!' I bark.

We turn a corner and suddenly Lake Walliss comes into view. It's vast, over 12,000 hectares, with more water than Sydney Harbour, according to Google.

The lake is almost monocoloured, all white and grey, reflecting the dark sky. The surface is churning with waves, whipped up by the strong winds. It looks relentless, like a real force of nature. In the far distance I can see a few jetties stretching out from the other edge of the lake, toward the mountains. But on our side is only one jetty, with a solitary houseboat moored there. It's about the size of a shipping container, but it looks more like a glass box sitting on a fibreglass base, with a kind of deck on the top. Two banana lounges on the deck drunkenly slide back and forth with the wind.

Three trails snake outward from the lake. One to the right of the water leads down to the jetty with the houseboat, while the one to the left leads to a caravan park. A third trail in the middle winds up into the hills beyond the lake, which is where we're headed, according to what Google Maps showed us before we lost signal.

The hills are covered in dense bushland, the trees bending reluctantly with the winds coming off the water. Even at this time of day, parts of the hills are shrouded in a ghostly mist.

Ahead of us is a small general store next to a white boom gate with red diagonal 'warning' stripes on it, sitting across a dramatic dip between the main road and the rest of the area. There's a rusty box on a pole just before the gate with an analogue keypad. It seems that going through the gate is the only way to access the lake, or the caravan park, or the other trail that we are meant to follow to find The Circle. There's no other way in or out, as far as I can tell.

A large sign outside the store reads 'All visitors register here for gate access'. There are other smaller signs peppering the walls of the store, listing all the things they sell, from food and beer to fishing gear and bait.

As soon as we climb out of the car the winds hit us full force. I feel instantly cold, like someone has tipped a bag of ice over me. But my stomach feels better, so that's something. I stretch my legs and stare across the lake. The water level is low from the dry summer we've had. Near the lake's edge I can see a couple of tree branches sticking out of the water, between the chopping waves. At least you can see them. It's the stuff under the surface, the stuff you can't see, that is the real danger.

Like Mum and me. At night I watch her drinking wine, staring into space, beyond the house, beyond our life. I don't know what she's seeing, but it hurts her. Maybe it's just remembering the accident that mangled her legs? All I know is that sometimes it feels like my life is like these sticks in the lake – something treacherous that has to be carefully navigated.

While Kane stretches his legs and Shell collects our rubbish, I head toward the store, noting a pile of hessian sandbags lined up near the door as I do. Just how bad is this storm expected to be?

A buzzer goes off somewhere as I open the door. Inside, it's like stepping back in time. The place is cluttered but has a rustic charm. The wooden counter is well-worn, stained with years of use, covered with fishing magazines, several dirty coffee cups and a full ashtray. There's an ancient cash register sitting next to an EFTPOS machine.

The walls are adorned with a mix of photos of local fishermen holding their catches up with pride, as well as old footy posters and beer coasters. Over in one corner, there's a section where you can get fishing gear like rods and reels, tackle boxes brimming with hooks, sinkers and lures. There's also a few Eskys and a big fridge full of beers and soft drinks. I spot Cheezels on one of the shelves, grinning as I grab a box.

Behind the counter is a door covered in colourful strips of plastic. A short man with a long grey beard and dark, suspicious eyes emerges, parting the long strips like curtains.

'You here for the southern lights? I'd give it a miss if I were you mate, with this storm.'

'Uh, no, I don't know what that is. Me and my friends have to get to The Circle. Is it through that gate over there?'

He looks me up and down like I'm an alien. 'Name?'

'Angus Green.'

From his pocket he takes out an ancient iPhone. He scrolls his nicotine-stained finger along the screen. 'Right, Angus. I got an email saying you were coming and to give you access.'

Sliding his phone back in his pocket with one hand, he scribbles a code on a yellow Post-it and hands it to me with the other. 'Use this code to get through the gate, then take the middle trail. The Circle is high up on the hill.'

'Can I just ask, who did you get the email from?' *Who knew we were coming?*

'You don't know who sent it?' He takes out his phone again and looks closely at the screen. 'It's from The Circle's generic email address, so it could have been any of them.'

'No, I don't know who sent it, or who I'm meant to meet there.'

He stares at me. 'Well, they're all nutters up there . . . if I was you, I'd turn around now while you can.'

I pay for the Cheezels, thank him and head to the door.

'Well, if you're still going, make sure you got somewhere to stay up there. And park the car as high up on the hill as you can. The mother of all storms is hitting tonight. It's gonna flood here. Tell those Circle twits that Vince said everyone down here by the jetty and the caravan park has already left to sit it out in town till it passes, and they should too. Tell them I'm the last one to leave.'

Vince follows me to the door and reaches to turn the 'Open' sign around to 'Closed'. With that, he shuffles back through the doorway he emerged from, another crinkling noise of plastic strips the only thing suggesting he'd been there at all.

Post-it note in hand, I walk outside and back to the car.

'The guy in the shop said this storm is going to be massive. He said that everyone's left except for the people at The Circle and that we should turn back while we still can.'

'Great,' says Kane sarcastically as he slides back into the driver's seat. 'We really should have listened to your mum, Gus.'

'They wouldn't have stayed unless they were prepared for a storm, right?' Shell asks, pulling her beanie a little tighter onto her head before climbing back into the car.

'Who knows. But get this: someone told the bloke in the shop that we were coming. He gave me this code to get through the gate,' I reply.

Shell leans over from the back seat. 'Who told him we were coming?'

'He doesn't know. He was sent a message from a generic email.'

Vince comes out of the shop carrying a huge duffle bag, which he throws into the back of his battered silver ute, then he starts to push the heavy-looking sandbags up against the front door and windows. One by one, building a barrier.

Even I can see that it's a bit of natural valley here, a plateau between the lake lower down and the caravan park and everything else that's higher up. The shop and the road would really be susceptible to flooding. No wonder he's bagging up and getting out.

Kane drives to the boom gate and I read out the code for him to tap into the grimy keypad. When the boom gate goes up, he drives through and we start to take the trail to the community up a very rough, uphill dirt track. In the rear-view mirror I spot Vince taking off in his ute. He said he was the last one to leave. We're all alone now, except for whoever is at The Circle.

Chapter 4

Shovel

After about five minutes of careful off-road driving, going up and up, we arrive at a round sign that looks like a rubbish bin lid, with 'The Circle' spray-painted on it. If you weren't looking for it, you'd never find it, jammed next to a hedge.

Past the sign there are six ramshackle cabins about twenty metres apart from each other in a rough kind of circle on a big block of land. The left and rear of the area are surrounded by dense bushland. To the right of the cabins, there is a side trail leading down to the lake, maybe ten minutes' walk away.

The cabins are boxy, each with a verandah, a big front window, and a number from one to six painted in black next to the door. The front doors are fitted with that retro ribbed glass that distorts everything, which I like. Black solar panels gleam on each roof, and big water tanks nestle against their side walls. There's something unbalanced about the cabins, looking at them front-on. It takes me a second to realise that the cabins on the left seem to be larger than the ones on the right.

There's a massive garden with veggies and some flowers along the left-hand side of the block, next to a compost mound. Beyond that there's a small shed which I think houses a generator, judging by the cables running from the shed to each of the cabins. On the right-hand side is another shed, but much bigger, with a couple of lift-up garage doors.

Of much more interest, further up on the hill, is a formation of stones in a circle that must give The Circle its name. The stones are tall and ancient, like Stonehenge, but not as big, from what I can tell. From a distance, they almost look like a group of people standing or crouched in a strange, twisted circular formation. Each stone varies in height and shape, but you can tell these stones were placed there deliberately, not just a random occurrence. They look to be a short walk further up the hill behind the cabins.

Maybe it's the dark, stormy sky, but there's something spooky and mysterious and kinda mesmerising about the stones. What's their story, I wonder?

Out the front of the cabin closest to the road, several people are arranging sandbags in front and around the doorway and the edge of the verandah. A wheelbarrow positioned next to them is piled high with sand.

As we pull up, Kane bashes the car horn. A loud AC/DC riff plays, to Shell's and my total embarrassment.

'What did you do that for?' Shell snaps.

'Just getting their attention,' Kane snickers.

As the horn goes off, the group look up at us, scowling like a nineties album cover. I count four of them, two middle-aged women, and a teenage girl and guy.

The three of us look at each other. Shell's eyebrows are high. Kane's mouth is open goofily. And I'm just thinking neither of these women look like the pictures of Jane I've seen in the media from twelve years ago. Even accounting for aging or weight gain, neither could remotely be her.

At the centre of this crew is a short but imposing woman in her late forties or early fifties, with pale, freckled skin and long, vivid red hair in a rough ponytail, framing a strong face and intelligent-looking eyes. She's wearing a green jumper and old jeans, with a shovel in her hands, which she must have been using to move sand from the wheelbarrow into the sandbags. Everyone seems to be looking at us and then to her and us again. She's clearly the one in charge.

As she looks us up and down, I swear she's holding the shovel like it's a weapon.

'What do you want?' says the young guy, who looks my age. He has red hair, tight and curly, with pale skin and freckles like the boss woman. *Her son?* He's glaring at us for some reason. He's scary, but also kind of hot in his death metal long-sleeve T-shirt, ripped jeans and black biker boots. I realise I have been staring at him too long.

Next to him is a strange-looking girl, maybe nineteen or twenty, with shortly cropped brown hair and super thick glasses that make her eyes look huge, like a human owl. She seems to blink really slowly. She's wearing ripped orange overalls, a pink 'Little Miss Happy' T-shirt, and a bulky blue woollen cardigan.

'Who are you?' says the other woman. She's probably in her late thirties with dyed, dirty blonde hair and a full face of makeup, despite being in the middle of nowhere. Her dark roots make her look like a skunk in reverse. Her leopard-skin patterned top strains against her large chest, which is transfixing Kane. I'm more distracted by her hoop earrings, which a small budgie could easily use as a swing.

The guy from the shop was right; they are a weird group.

Suddenly a flash of lightning cracks the sky. We all jump. Even though I'm on edge and feeling nervy, I step forward a little. 'Hi, my name is Angus Green. These are my friends Shell and Kane. I'm looking for a woman called Jane Winter. Someone told me I could find her here.'

'Who told you she was here?' It's the boss woman, staring directly at me, still holding the shovel like she might hit something with it.

I gulp. 'I don't actually know. I was sent an anonymous message saying she was here. She's my birth mother.'

I get the screenshot I took of the message up on my phone and walk up to the scary shovel-woman to show her. Wiping her hands on her jeans, she holds it very close to her eyes before shaking her head and handing it back.

'Okay, well maybe you recognise her?' I pass her my phone again, showing a photo of Jane from one of the old media articles.

The woman holds up the phone to the others. They all shake their heads, saying they don't recognise her. I can't explain why, but I don't believe them. One of them knows something. It's like I can sense exchanged glances taking place just out of my eyeline. Like the silence is somehow curated.

I step back, closer to Kane and Shell. *Back to safety,* I can't help but think. While I've been talking to the group, Shell's been forensically studying them. She touches my arm and whispers, 'None of these women could be Jane. Not even with *major* surgery.'

'I know,' I whisper back.

'What do we do now?' asks Kane softly. 'We should probably get going.' He points upwards at the ever-darkening sky.

As if on cue, it starts raining.

From out of the shadow of one of the cabins set further back in the clearing, a short, thin man who looks to be in his late forties emerges. 'There is an enormous storm about to hit. Where are you staying?' His voice is deep and quiet, posh yet vaguely sinister. He's dressed like a university professor in a collared shirt, a tweed jacket, proper pants and old brown brogues, but with a blue baseball cap, which is an odd touch.

The three of us look at each other, and Kane shrugs. Suddenly the rain intensifies, pelting our faces. I want to run under the verandah for cover, but it's clear that we are not exactly welcome here.

'You may not make it back to town. There is a spare cabin here if you want to sit out the storm for the night.' He points toward another cabin at the back of the block, marked 'six'.

The boss woman glares at him. His baseball cap is pulled down low but when he looks up at her I can see an eye patch over his left eye. They seem to have a conversation without words before he looks directly at us. I can't read his face. Is he fearing our discomfort? Or enjoying it?

'Pirate,' mutters Kane.

'Oh,' says Shell, more sympathetically.

I don't want to spend time with this strange group, but that message about Jane brought me here, so I don't want to leave either. I'm not sure what to do.

'If you're going, you better go now, before the road by the boom gate floods,' adds the boss woman, eyeing us up and down. The young guy near her sneers his agreement.

Kane leans in to Shell and me, talking quietly. 'She's right. We should go now, before the rain gets worse.' He's looking at his Kingswood with a concerned face. 'The car will be hard to manoeuvre if it does flood.'

'If we can't drive back to Melbourne in the storm, we're going to have to stay somewhere. If we don't stay here, where do we stay?' Shell points out quite reasonably.

'The caravan park up the other trail?' I suggest. It sounded like Vince at the shop said everyone had left, so I'm not sure there will be anyone there. But if we could stay there, then we're still close enough in case Jane turns up here. Why can't Kane see that I need to stay here, or at least *near* here?

The rain starts to get even heavier. I shudder at the thought of being caught in this.

'Get out of the rain,' says the girl with the big glasses, waving us to join them under the large verandah. We gratefully move to shelter.

Shell steps forward and holds out her hand to the boss woman.

'I'm Shell, and the muscle tragic is Kane,' she says with a smirk, pointing at Kane.

The woman shakes Shell's hand. 'Cath,' she says, then points to everyone in turn. 'This is my son Nash, that's Maxine in the leopard top, Greta in the overalls, and Tobias in the cap.'

We nod at each other as they're introduced. I notice Maxine ogling Kane in his now wet T-shirt and shorts and hi-top gym boots. Even if he was freezing, he'd never let on.

'Oh shit,' Maxine mutters, looking past the three of us. 'Walker's coming back.'

She points a blood-red painted fingernail back toward the road, where an ostentatiously large and shiny four-wheel drive is coming around the bend.

Kane whistles, impressed. 'A Mercedes-Maybach GLS 600 V8! Wow.'

'Eh?' I say. *It's certainly mint, but who cares?*

The four-wheel drive pulls up near the sign, behind the Kingswood. Out steps a very tall, handsome, slick-looking man. He looks like he should be a TV newsreader or gameshow host with his perfect hair, tanned skin and expensive suit perfectly tailored to his lean body. As he opens up an umbrella with the seamless flick of a button, there's a flash at his wrist, where I can see that he is wearing a huge, fancy metal wristwatch.

There is an air about him. He is *someone.*

We all stare at him.

Shell says, 'I want his eyebrows.'

Kane says, 'I want his car.'

I say, 'I want his watch.'

He grins wolfishly at Cath and the others. 'Getting ready for the end of the world?'

Chapter 5

Jacket

Cath plants the shovel into the sand and puts her hands firmly on her hips. 'Go away Simon, I've got nothing more to say to you now,' she says, staring him down.

He stops a few steps away, umbrella in one hand, the other raised palm-up in a *I come in peace* gesture. He seems to tower over the Circle residents. Compared to them he's like a powerful giant that could crush them.

'This storm is going to be biblical. It will wash your resolve away, Cath.' He smiles at her, doing that one eyebrow raise thing that I can never do. He is very cocky in an annoyingly attractive way. His voice is deep and persuasive.

Greta stomps toward him in the rain. 'No one wants you here, Walker.'

'Come now, that's rude, even for you.' He puts one hand on his hip in mock-offense while the other arm keeps his umbrella firmly in place. The rain falls around him, as if he is immune.

Greta points a finger back at him. 'We're gonna protect our land and our circle. You can't just take it.' Her voice shakes in fury.

He smirks at her. 'But you can't say "our" land when it's Cath's land. She owns it, unlike you or any of you other hangers-on.'

'We're a community,' Cath says, squaring her shoulders, making her seem suddenly taller and stronger. 'And we all have a stake in this land.'

Walker keeps going, grinning at them as he walks a little back and forth, as if giving a lecture. 'This would be a very suitable site for an extension of the caravan park. And that stone circle would make an amazing tourist attraction, a real money spinner.' He adjusts the sparkling watch on his wrist and makes a cash register *ka-ching* noise.

Greta grips her overall straps, her chin low, like a kid sulking. 'The stone circle is magic, it's gotta be protected.'

Maxine comes up and puts her arms around Greta's shoulders. 'Ignore him, luv,' she says softly. Greta relaxes into her embrace. They come back under the verandah for cover, shoes already squelching as the heavy rain is already starting to turn the ground into mud.

Maxine turns her attention to Walker. 'Just piss off, would you? The land and the circle are not for sale.'

Walker shakes his head and looks to Cath. 'You will sell me this land.' He smiles as he speaks, but I can see the steel in his eyes, and his hand clenches in a fist. 'Or I will tell this lot your *big* secret . . .'

Cath's mouth drops open. She goes to speak but stops herself, her face flushed.

Suddenly a splash of wet sand hits Walker's face, and he drops the umbrella in surprise. Recovering quickly, he pulls a silk hanky from his pocket and wipes the sand from his eyes. When he picks up the umbrella again he points it at Nash like it's a gun.

'You little idiot,' he snarls as Nash unashamedly wipes his dirty hands on his already filthy jeans. 'Is that all you've got? You think you're some kind of hard man, but you're just a weak little kid.'

Nash's pale skin burns red. Cath grabs his arm before he can react. 'Stop. He's just trying to get a rise out of you.'

'You . . . shit!' shouts Greta.

Walker throws his head back and laughs mockingly. 'Oh, I'm mortally wounded.' He makes a stabbed-in-the-heart gesture and pretends to recoil a little before narrowing his eyes at Greta. 'Cath only keeps you here out of pity. You're like a three-legged cat. Once I buy this land, you'll be out on your arse!'

Maxine tightens her arms around Greta, whose bottom lip drops as she looks back at Cath in desperation. Cath shakes her head. 'Ignore him, you know that's not true.'

Greta still looks hurt.

Maxine raises her finger to point at Walker. 'You're a nasty piece of work, aren't you? Even if she wanted to leave The Circle, Cath would never sell to the likes of you!'

The gesture might have had more impact if her fake fingernail hadn't fallen off as she jabbed at him.

Walker's nostrils flare like a horse. 'I hope you have plenty of booze stored up, Maxine. With this storm it might be days before you can get to the bottle shop again. There's a real danger you may actually get sober enough to remember what you did. Or should I tell everyone now?'

Maxine recoils. 'You bastard!'

Wow, he's going round ripping shreds off everyone, one by one, like targets in a shooting gallery.

From behind us, Tobias steps forward. 'That is enough! We all know you would say anything to make this sale, you fraud.' His voice is hard with control.

'What did you call me, freak?' snarls Walker.

There is a sudden silence, like time itself has stopped. We're all looking at Tobias, waiting for a response.

'Be careful with what you say.' Tobias speaks quietly, but there's ice in his voice.

Walker holds his ground, smirk still in place. 'I know more about you than you might think, you know. What are you going to do? Sacrifice me to some pagan gods in your precious stone circle under the southern lights?'

Tobias stares intensely at Walker, like he's boring into his soul. Somehow this seems more powerful with only one eye. 'The circle is unique, and it will be heritage protected soon,' he says evenly. A sliver of a smile comes to his mouth, a twitching of his top lip, just perceptible in the rain. With that chillingly even tone, he continues. 'Does your father know you're trying to harass Cath into selling?'

Walker looks back angrily but says nothing this time. He crosses his free arm across his chest protectively.

Tobias keeps going. 'Did he bully you as a child? Did he call you worthless?'

Walker's mouth forms a harsh slit. His eyes burn with something violent. Tobias has clearly touched a nerve.

Tobias sees this and keeps going. 'Your father is a very successful businessman who thinks you are a failure. The last owner would not sell to him, would she? If you managed to buy this land, if you succeeded where he could not, you could prove him wrong. It's your last big chance to show that you have what it takes, isn't it? You have more to lose than any of us.'

Cath puts her hands out between Walker and the others. 'Let's everyone just calm down. The storm is starting in earnest. Simon, just leave, *please*. Go back to town while you still can, before the road out floods completely.'

He goes to respond to Cath, then suddenly seems to register me and Shell and Kane. 'Who the hell are you lot?'

Flustered, I stammer, 'I . . . I'm here looking for a woman called Jane.'

He looks puzzled.

I scramble out into the rain to show him the photo. He doesn't offer me cover under his umbrella, so I shove the phone in front of him. His eyebrows go up for a moment and my heart skips a beat. 'Do you know her?'

He looks past me, smirking. 'Why are you looking for her?'

He knows her! I feel panicky. 'Have you seen her? She's my mother.'

The smirk quickly fades from his face. He turns away, collapses his umbrella and swiftly climbs back into his car, avoiding my eye.

'Hey,' I call out, desperation in my voice. 'Do you know her? Where is she? Did *you* send me the message?'

He starts the car and throttles the engine. Even his four-wheel drive struggles to turn around in the wet turf. A jet of water flies in the air as he speeds off into the distance.

I don't know what to say. I look at Shell and Kane. He must know her, or of her at least, based on his weird reaction to her photo. I just wish he hadn't sped off without telling me what his connection is with Jane.

What does he know? I quickly bolt back under cover, my mind churning.

Shell looks to Cath. 'Can we call him or something?'

Cath dips her head. 'I can give you his number, but there's no reception here right now. Maybe in the morning, once the storm passes.'

'We have to stay now,' I say quietly to the others. They both nod.

Kane's looking back the way we came, where the puddling rain is quickly creating multiple mini lakes on the road. 'Yeah, I reckon the Kingswood might just sink. It's not built like his beast.'

'That settles it then,' Shell says. She turns to Cath and then to Tobias. 'If the offer still stands, yes, we'd like to stay in your spare cabin. Just till this storm passes.'

Maxine claps her hands, her nails clacking. 'You should come to Cath's fiftieth tonight. We're still going to have our party, aren't we?' She asks with a hint of desperation, her hands shaking. I wonder if Walker was right about her drinking.

Cath relaxes her stance. 'Yes, why should we let the storm stop us?

Right then, let's get you kids sorted. Nash, get the key for cabin six please.'

Nash frowns but stomps past us into cabin one, which must belong to him and Cath.

Cath looks back at us. 'Number six only has one bedroom, I'm afraid, but there's a couch big enough to sleep on.' Then she turns to Greta. 'Do you think you can turn their power on?' Greta nods, beaming with the attention.

Cath gestures past Kane to the Kingswood. 'You'll need to move your car higher up the hill, near the garage. Less chance of it sinking there.'

These arrangements are all fine, but I desperately want to know what Walker knows about Jane. 'Cath, do you know why that Walker guy would know my mother? Any idea at all?'

She shakes her head. Funny, but I don't believe her. Something in her expression isn't right. And I think she can tell that I'm not buying it.

Nash emerges from the cabin with the key on a ring with a plastic tag marked 'six'. He goes to hand it to me, but then makes a point of handing it to Shell instead. Weird.

Kane runs back to the car and puts it in gear. The wheels turn uselessly in the sodden path until he floors it and eventually manages to take off up the hill, water flying everywhere.

Cath hands Shell and me a couple of umbrellas from a cylindrical container by her front door. She gives me a pink one and Shell a blue one, which is funny. She reaches behind the container and produces a large red torch, which she hands to me.

'You might need this till the power comes back on. It'll be cold, but there should be blankets and bedding still in the bedroom wardrobe.'

Cath pulls a couple of black rain jackets with hoods from a

collection hanging on hooks by the door. She sees me looking at them. I must look confused because she says, 'I bought a job lot of these on sale. Everyone, take one and put these on while we finish the sandbags.'

Everyone grabs a jacket from her, and I take one extra for Kane.

'We're starting the party at six,' giggles Maxine, staring at Kane's car in the distance, struggling to do her jacket up over her chest. 'A party in a storm will be fun.'

Chapter 6

Generator

I find myself staring at Greta. She seems oddly innocent and childlike, even though she's a couple of years older than us. I can tell that Shell is intrigued by her too.

'I'll have to check the generator before we can get your power up,' says Greta. 'The output's a bit patchy. Timing mechanism's probably a bit out of whack.'

'How do you know how to fix it?' Shell asks.

Greta smiles. 'My dad was an engineer and could fix anything. He taught me.'

I want to ask where her family is now, and why she's living in this community, but figure there will be time to find out things later.

'Can I come along? I'm really interested in how things work,' Shell asks.

Greta looks at her all wide-eyed. 'Sure! I'll just get my toolbox.' She dashes off in the rain toward the cabin marked 'three'.

I look around and take in the cabins again. I guess I was right about some of the cabins being bigger than the others, since Cath and Nash must live in cabin one, which clearly has two bedrooms, unlike cabin six, where we'll be staying. It makes me wonder who is in the others. Greta is opening the door to cabin three, so that must be hers. Assuming Tobias and Maxine are in separate cabins, that leaves another cabin unaccounted for. I wonder who lives, or lived, there?

I notice Shell watching Greta go into cabin three.

'What are you doing?' I ask, grinning.

She frowns at me. 'What?'

'Is this you flirting? Most people would use flattery or whatever, not watch someone fix a generator! Very butch.'

Her face goes red and I can see she's embarrassed, which is not something that happens often.

'No, that's not it.'

I poke her in the arm. 'You like her, don't you?'

'No, I'm just interested in . . . how people fix things.'

'Since when?'

'Since always.'

'I don't believe you.'

'Piss off,' Shell storms off toward the shed with the generator, her boots squelching in the mud.

I spot Greta dashing from cabin three with her toolbox toward the generator shed. She has this vague look on her face, like she's just on the cusp of being here, but somewhere else as well.

Why is Shell being so weird? I pull my jacket closed and run to the verandah of another cabin, just close enough to see what they're doing, but not be noticed.

The generator shed is about the size of a single-car garage, made out of dark green Colourbond. When Greta opens the door I can see that the generator takes up most of the available space. It's a solid, industrial-looking machine with cords running to the roof, which is sitting on an elevated steel frame, with some kind of wind turbine on the side. The massive fan is churning away but at a stuttering speed, like something is not quite right.

'We all have solar panels to run basic power and stuff like our fridges. We also have this backup diesel generator for the rest,' Greta shouts over the sound of the generator and the rain.

Shell nods enthusiastically. 'Very sustainable.'

'Now I can hear it properly, the timing is off, yeah,' says Greta. She rummages around in her toolbox and takes out a wrench. 'Turn that power button off, will you? Need to power down before I do anything.'

They both stare at the generator, waiting for it to wind down. I wish I could wind down my brain that easily. All I can think about is why someone would get me to come all the way out here to this weird campground in the middle of nowhere, especially since nobody here knows who Jane is. Or at least that's what they're saying. I don't know about all of them, but Cath is definitely lying. She knows something. So does Walker. I wish I could contact him right now and find out what he knows.

For all I know, Jane could be hiding here somewhere, watching me. But if she's here, then where? Why not come out and meet me? I look around the area again, as if I might somehow catch a glimpse of her out the corner of my eye, peering through binoculars from a window, like in a TV show.

'I like how eco-focused your community is,' Shell says, pointing to the rows of veggies and flowers, and a very established-looking compost pile.

Greta fiddles with a switch on the generator. 'Yeah, the environment matters lots when you live here. You become mates with nature. We use tank water for everything. Even the dunny has a cassette under it so we can use our own waste to fertilise the garden.'

Ew. If I go near that garden, I will not be breathing in.

The concept of 'mates with nature' resonates with Shell, who has been running sustainability programs at our school. She nods enthusiastically, clearly in her element.

I'm far from mine. This is as boring as a day with no internet access.

I look around and see Kane running toward Maxine, who is standing outside cabin two, waving to him. As they talk, her face is very expressive and flirty. She gets him filling and lugging sandbags across her cabin door. He seems to be moving them easier than the guy from the shop was. I guess his endless gym work is paying off today. Impressive, given last year he was limping about after a knee reconstruction.

I edge closer so I can hear them more clearly. I know I'm being creepy, listening in on Shell and Kane's conversations, but I'm really curious about these people. One of them might reveal something about Jane.

'It's so nice living away from the big city here. We can do what we want, see who we want. No rules. Anything goes.' I think she's winking at Kane. He grins at her. This is embarrassingly cringe, but I can't look away.

'So how old are you, Keith?'

'It's Kane. I'm nineteen.'

She laughs. 'Oops, sorry luv.'

Even from here I can see that her eyes are bloodshot. Mum's used to be like that when she was drinking a lot.

Kane puts down his latest sandbag and wipes his forehead with the hem of his T-shirt, revealing his sixpack. This is a typical Kane move these days. His socials are full of pictures of him pulling the same pose. Maxine certainly enjoys the view. 'Oh, you could grate cheese on that!' she giggles, poking his stomach lightly. He pulls his shirt down, making out it was an accident that his shirt rode up at all, but I can tell his brain is ticking over. A video of him doing this will no doubt appear on his socials once we get back home. Everything is content now, I guess.

Chapter 7

Knife

Suddenly Nash appears at Maxine's verandah.

'Hurry up, we need to do Tobias's cabin next, then the others.' I didn't even see him approach. Kane bristles a bit at being told what to do, but doesn't say anything, which is unusual for him. Maxine looks annoyed that Nash is taking Kane away and frowns at him, crossing her arms over her chest.

I bolt over to cabin two and offer to help. Nash nods. 'You can help me with Tobias's, and Kane can do Greta's.'

Kane heads over to cabin three, and Nash and I run to cabin five. Tobias meets us at the front door and we all grab nearby shovels and start filling the bags with sand from a pile near the bottom step.

'Do you go to school or uni?' I ask Nash. There's something about him that draws me in. I want to know everything about him, even though he's not exactly welcoming my attention.

'Nup,' he grunts.

Well, that doesn't give me much to go on.

'That's cool, I guess.'

'What's cool about it?' he says dryly.

'Um, well, I thought no school would be good,' I stutter. *God, how embarrassing.*

He snorts and sticks his hands in his overall pockets. 'Living in this shithole isn't though. There's nothing to do, nowhere to go. I can't wait to get away from here.'

Now that he says it, I guess I would sooner be at school and living in the city than out here in the middle of nowhere, with a bunch of strange people and my mum.

'How long have you been living out here?' I ask.

'We moved here a couple of years ago. Mum wanted to get away from the city, the bullshit. She was a real estate agent, so it was easy for her to find this place.'

When he's not frowning, his face is quite handsome, in a rough kind of way. He looks like a lost dog who needs help, but also like one that might bite at any minute.

As he leans over the sand pile, a Swiss Army Knife falls out of his back pocket.

Tobias points to the ground. 'Nash, you dropped your knife.'

'I have one of those,' I say. 'I take it everywhere.' *What am I saying? Why am I talking at all?*

'Why?' Nash picks the knife up and pockets it.

'Why what?'

'Why do you take it everywhere?'

I don't know how to answer. I can't tell him I used to use it to cut myself when I felt overwhelmed by the world. Now doesn't seem the right time to mention my self-harm issues. I wish I hadn't said anything. Very clumsily, I try to change the subject.

'Anyway, if you think this place is so bad, why do you stay?'

Nash looks angry all of a sudden. 'None of your business mate,' he spits. 'Move your big arse, I need to get there next.'

Ouch. We can't all be lean like him or jacked like Kane. I pull my jacket more closely around me, trying to cover up. He sees this and for a moment something flashes over his face . . . regret? But then it's gone.

I awkwardly move aside as he puts a second bag in place in front of the door.

'Don't be rude, Nash,' says Tobias, lugging a third bag in place.

'Don't tell me what to do, Professor,' Nash snaps back. 'Fill up that one,' Nash says, pointing to the last bag sitting by the verandah.

I grab a spade and fill it up with sand. When I go to lift it, it's much heavier than I expect, and I drop it. Sand spills out all over my feet.

Nash sighs. 'You're supposed to only half fill them so you can carry them.'

Embarrassed, I start to scoop the sand back into the bag with my hands, avoiding his eyes. Eventually I manage to drag it over to Nash without making myself look like an idiot.

When I look up, Tobias is watching me. Studying me, more accurately. I'm about to say something when there's a massive crack of thunder and the rain starts absolutely barrelling down, even heavier than before. We all snap out of whatever we were snapped into and look to the sky.

Cath appears from around the corner and shepherds us under the verandah. 'I hope we've made the right decision to stay,' she says, almost to herself. She does look worried. Her heavily lidded eyes stare past the horizon, like's she's trying to see into the future.

'Have you had bad storms up here before?' I ask.

She looks back at me, still a little suspicious. 'Yes, but not as bad as the bureau is predicting this time.'

'We're nearly ready Mum, I just need to check Greta's place was done right and then finish bagging cabin four. The strangers can do their own,' Nash says, arms spread wide as he indicates all the sandbags. Funny that he refers to us as 'strangers', like we're the ones being all weird and cagey.

'Who's in cabin four?' I ask.

Cath glances at Tobias before answering. 'John, an artist. He went away early this morning. We were expecting him back for the party but he must have been delayed with this rain.'

'Could he know something about Jane?' I push.

'You can ask him yourself. He'll be back tomorrow,' Cath says curtly. She really knows how to shut a conversation down. She and Nash have that in common.

Greta and Shell come up the verandah steps, their jackets dripping. 'I've fixed the generator's timing, and the power is on in cabin six,' says Greta. There's an element of neediness in her voice and face, like she's a puppy wanting to be patted. Cath touches her shoulder and smiles, which I guess is the human equivalent.

Suddenly a monstrous bolt of lightning flashes across the sky and lights up the stone circle. Greta screams. Shell and I look at each other in surprise.

Cath draws Greta close. 'Greta is really scared of lightning, aren't you?'

Greta nods. I notice Nash rolling his eyes.

'She was grazed by it as a kid.'

Greta's bottom lip wobbles. 'I was paralysed for a week. My whole body went into shock, it was depolarised or something. I hate lightning and storms.' Her voice goes higher as she talks, clearly still traumatised.

Maxine and Kane run up the steps. Kane's drenched shirt is glued to his body. He shakes himself down, and, noticing how his shirt is clinging to him, shamelessly takes his phone out of his pocket and snaps a selfie. He's so cringe sometimes.

Cath takes charge again. 'Greta, go and finish your cabin with Tobias, then get him to help you finish at Maxine's. Nash, can you manage number four by yourself?'

Nash grunts and sets off into the rain. Cath turns back to us.

'You kids will have to do your own cabin. Take what's left in the wheelbarrow.'

We race over to cabin six and spend the next twenty minutes sandbagging, getting soaked to the bone.

Chapter 8

Stones

After we've done the sandbags, we run over to Kane's car, parked near the garage, and grab our stuff out of the boot. The rain is getting worse by the minute. The others seem to have all gone back into their cabins and an unnerving calm has come across the block, even as the rain torrents down.

We stand under the verandah with our bags, listening to the rain pelting heavily onto the tin roof.

'It's stunning here,' says Shell, standing beside me, staring out at the bush to one side of us and the lake on the other. 'Elemental.' She's taking in deep breaths, stretching her arms out, accidentally bumping Kane in the bicep as she goes.

'Careful, don't touch the goods,' he snickers. He's got his phone out and is taking pics of himself flexing in front of this vista, with the lake in the background.

He's relentless these days. I feel like I see some part of his body on socials every day. He's trying to get some kind of sponsorship or collab with some aligned brand, like protein shakes or gym gear or whatever. I mean I get it. He hasn't had a job since he left high school and some people seem to make plenty of money through social media, but still. It's like he's a different person sometimes.

'Don't you ever get tired of looking at yourself?' asks Shell as she pulls the cabin key from her pocket.

'Not when there's this much to enjoy,' he laughs.

'Maybe you should have chronicled our last investigation, instead of your muscle journey?' I suggest.

'Jealous much?' he flexes at me.

I yelp as the wind changes and the rain starts coming at us sideways. Shell turns the key and we almost burst through our cabin door, blown in by the wind. We chuck the umbrellas in the corner, hang our jackets by the door, and drop our bags on the floor.

The cabin is dark and cold and smells musty, but I'm glad to be out of the storm. Shell hits the light switch and the lights flicker briefly, then come to life. Thanks Greta. The warm light is a nice contrast to the blackening sky we can see through the windows as I pull the blinds up.

It's pretty basic, as expected. The main room we're in is an open-plan kitchen and lounge, very eighties. Beige on beige. There's an old floral-patterned couch, a bulky wooden coffee table, and a TV unit but no TV. The kitchen has a stove and a fridge, but the fridge door is open and there's nothing inside. There are two internal doors which I guess lead off into the bedroom and bathroom.

'It's a dump and it's freezing,' mutters Kane. I want to point out how little he's wearing, but I'm freezing too and I'm in jeans and a denim jacket with a thick shirt underneath. It is a dump, but as Mum would say, any port in a storm – in this case literally.

The bedroom is bare, other than a bed base topped with a mattress, and framed by a couple of bedside tables with ugly lamps sitting on them. Oh well, at least we don't have to sleep on the floor, and one of us can sleep on the couch.

'I'd open a window for some fresh air, but . . .' Shell gestures to the storm raging outside.

She opens the wardrobe door and, as promised, inside there's sheets and blankets and towels, all stored in clear plastic bags. They smell a bit musty but not too bad. We shake the bedclothes and hang them off a chair in the room to air out.

Kane flops across the couch, big feet hanging off the edge. 'You two can take the bedroom and I'll sleep on the couch. You guys are like a strange couple anyway.' Weird thing to say, but I remember that the last time we were away together, working our case, he felt left out. Shell and I are such a team, we can't help it. I wonder if that jealousy he felt back then is still a thing?

'Are you sure the couch is okay?' I ask, hoping he'll say yes.

He gives me a thumbs up.

I look at our gear dumped by the door. Kane has a big sports bag, Shell has a whole suitcase, and I have a fake leather backpack. We only packed for a night, so Shell's big suitcase seems excessive.

'What's in the big case, Baldy?' Kane asks. 'Wigs?' he laughs.

Shell gives him the bird. 'What's in yours? Roids?'

He snickers.

'Let's get out of these wet clothes,' I say. Shell passes around some towels from the bedroom and starts to dry her spiky hair. I go into the bathroom to change without anyone seeing my love handles. Shell goes into the bedroom, leaving Kane in the lounge.

Alone in the dark bathroom, I can't stop thinking about Walker's reaction to Jane's picture. It definitely seemed like he knew something. He was grinning, but then when I mentioned she was my mother, it wiped the smile right off his face. *Why?* It's like me wanting to find her went from something funny to something deadly serious. Did he know about me before? I feel like I'm in limbo. I wish I could call Dr Yamada right now. He's been great over the last few months, helping me manage my anxiety and talking to me when I feel myself falling back into my old self-harm cycles. I feel stressed knowing he's not a phone call away anymore, or at least not until we get reception back.

I dry myself as best I can and open my bag. What do you wear to the fiftieth of someone you've just met who lives off the grid with a bunch of kooky strangers by a mysterious stone circle? Seeing

I only have one other set of clothes, I don't really have a choice.

Once we've all changed into dry clothes, we hang our wet stuff up on the back of the metal kitchen chairs and sit together in the lounge room.

'I'm just gonna say it, those people are batshit, especially Greta,' says Kane, stretching out his legs and resting them on the coffee table.

'Who has a birthday party in the middle of a big storm?' adds Shell, eyeing Kane's feet. He takes them off the table.

'Nash looks like he's ready to kill someone,' I say. Shell smiles at me. 'What?' I ask.

'I think you like Nash . . .'

'No way, he's trouble.' I can feel myself blushing, so neither of them believes me.

'That guy with the eye patch is especially spooky,' says Kane, covering one of his own eyes with his hand.

'Don't be a dick,' I say.

There's a flash of lightning that suddenly lights up the stone circle through the window. It looks eerie yet mesmerising at the same time. I stand up and go to the window for a closer look. Despite the storm, the circle seems to have a luminescence around it. It looks powerful, like some kind of beacon in the storm.

'Gus, what's wrong?' Shell asks.

'Hey, Gus?' says Kane.

I hear them both but only faintly, like voices from another room. All I can do is stare at the circle.

Kane shakes me by the shoulders. 'Hey, don't you go all weird on me too!'

I feel myself snap back into the room. *Was Greta right? Does this circle have actual power?* I want to talk to Tobias and find out more about this circle. It feels like he knows more than he's letting on – about everything. It takes me a second to notice I'm shivering.

Chapter 9

Painting

Once we're all ready, Kane points out that it's only 5.30 pm – too early to go to the party. Shell says she's going down to cabin one anyway to see if Cath needs any help setting up. I wonder if she's really going to find Greta, but I could be wrong.

The storm howls like a monster as Shell dashes out the door.

Kane says he's going to rest up and lays down on the couch. I grab my jacket and an umbrella and run across to cabin five, which I now know is Tobias's cabin. Standing on his verandah, looking around, I wonder again if Jane is hiding somewhere nearby, watching me. My skin prickles.

I go round the back of his cabin and have a closer look at the stone circle again. The angle and steep incline of the hill behind the cabins make it seem like the circle is somehow watching over the community. I find myself squinting at it, realising that it never feels entirely in focus. It's like some kind of apparition, a flickering ghost from the past.

I try to count the stones. *One, two, three* . . . they blur as I count, like they're trying to trick me, slipping in and out of my grasp.

'Are you having trouble counting them?' It's Tobias. I jump with surprise. I didn't hear him approach. *How could he know that?*

'Yes. Must be the rain,' I say.

He shakes his head. 'They are like that on clear days too. They seem to evade analysis if you look right at them. The trick is to close one eye and look at them sideways, with your tongue out.'

What? 'Are you joking?'

'Try,' he replies, smiling innocently.

I squint my left eye and try to look at them from a different angle. Reluctantly I poke my tongue out.

Then I realise he's snickering. He's taking the piss.

I feel embarrassed and annoyed. I'm interested in his stupid stones. I thought that would get me some credit with him. Not sure why I want to have credit with him, but that's a whole other thing. He's like one of those teachers that push you hard so you want to impress them, but then feel super dense when you let them down.

'Come inside, you're getting wet,' he says, leading me around to the front door. I realise the cabins don't have a back door, which is odd.

His cabin is what you could call minimalist. It has the same kind of basic hand-me-down furniture that ours does, but beyond that, the place is almost bare. A laptop sits on a heavy wooden desk that is facing the side window, giving a good view of the stone circle. There are neat stacks of books either side of the laptop and a collection of pens and notebooks.

The only real decoration is a painting on the far wall. It's a dark and twisted and quite alien-looking landscape of the stone circle. The dark greens and blacks almost attack each other. I can't take my eyes off it. I swear the painting is screaming.

'Do you like that painting?' Tobias asks, following my gaze.

'Yes. No. Well, not "like", exactly. It's kinda scary, actually,' I say, shaking my head.

'It certainly is beautiful and terrible at the same time. It captures that unsettling aspect of the circle well. John from cabin four painted that.'

I look back at him. 'How many stones are there really?'

'Eight main ones. But you can see where there are smaller ones too, and what I call the keystone in the middle.'

'What was the circle for?'

Tobias stretches out his hands and puts them behind his head. 'That's one of the things I'm trying to find out. But my main focus has to be on getting the historical overlay placed on the circle first, so developers like Walker can't get their hands on it.'

He scratches under his eye patch.

'Sorry, it gets itchy.'

'Can I ask what happened to your eye?'

'Stabbed in a knife fight in a bar,' he says, straight-faced.

I stare at him, mouth open.

'I am joking. Cancer. I got a melanoma behind my eye. Very rare, but I am fine. Now get your umbrella and jacket.' Tobias makes a *walk this way* gesture with his thumb. We leave the cabin and start to walk up the hill toward the circle.

Suddenly Kane comes bounding up and mock tackles me for a non-existent footy, knocking the umbrella out of my hand. 'You can't investigate the stones without me, Goose.'

'Idiot,' I say as he musses my already messy hair and generally acts like a fool.

'So who put the stones here? Druids?' Kane asks. I love how Kane just comes out with this stuff, no filter.

'Given their age, First Nations peoples. We don't really have a culture of druids in this country,' Tobias replies dryly.

'Bummer. What's it for?' Kane goes on.

'I don't know yet. I have two main theories, but I have no evidence for them. Because there are no local Indigenous communities living around here anymore, and it was only rediscovered recently, its real purpose may have been forgotten. Another piece of history lost to colonisation.'

I'm intrigued. 'What are these two theories?'

Tobias rubs his chin. 'The first theory, and the one I believe, is that it could have been used for purification ceremonies.'

Woah, that's intense. 'Why purification? How does that work?'

'It's a ceremony using fire to symbolically cleanse people of their sins. I've recently been in contact with a First Nations academic – Professor Draper – from another region. She found an obscure reference to the stones being called "The Burning Stones" by her mob.'

'Why?' Kane asks.

'Kane, you ask questions like a child.'

'Best way to find out more is to ask questions. Sorry, would you like me to ask them in a fancy way? "Illuminate me, Professor, what does one ascertain from a title such as The Burning Stones?"'

'Okay, point taken,' admits Tobias, chuckling.

'So the spirit gets purified by fire as part of some ritual?' I ask.

'Yes, that's my interpretation.'

'But they don't literally burn people?' I ask.

'No, like I said, it's symbolic. Fire is used to cleanse the spirit. See that flat stone at the front there? That's the keystone I mentioned. I think that is where you stand the person to be purified, and light the fire around them.'

'Wild. What's the other theory?' I ask. *This is pretty cool, actually.*

'That the circle was used to map the stars and the seasons. If you stand on a certain angle and look at the stones, you can see how they seem to line up with the mountain peaks in the distance and the stars at night. But there are not any official records of the circle, and First Nations groups passed knowledge through storytelling, rather than paper records. This is all guesswork on my part, which is why I have invited Professor Draper to inspect the stones when her teaching finishes this semester.'

'Could it be both for purification and for mapping the seasons?' I ask.

Tobias smiles a little. 'I have wondered that myself.'

Kane laughs. 'There was a stone circle in *Doctor Who*. The stones were actually blood sucking aliens left to guard a spaceship hidden in hyperspace just above the circle.'

'Yes, I am familiar with those episodes,' Tobias sighs.

'You like *Doctor Who*?' I ask, surprised and secretly pleased.

'No, but of course I am au fait with popular culture featuring stone circles. They have fascinated mankind for centuries.'

We walk in silence for a few minutes, umbrellas blasted with rain and wind. Out of nowhere, the mist that had settled around us earlier seems to fade away and the stones appear large before us. I find myself mesmerised by the circle again. Like it's drawing me to it.

'The stones will look amazing on Sunday night when the aurora australis – the southern lights – appear,' Tobias says.

'What are they?' Kane asks.

'Auroras appear to the naked eye as lines or ribbons of light across the night sky. They are caused by events such as solar flares across our southern polar region. In Victoria, they are visible roughly every eleven or twelve years, with the next ones due this Monday night. I'm looking forward to it. I just hope this storm has passed by then, otherwise we might not be able to see it.'

Suddenly a bolt of lightning strikes one of the stones, lighting them up dramatically in the darkening sky. It makes us all jump. Is the electricity in the air from the lightning, or is it from the stones?

'Let's get back inside. You should head over to the party,' says Tobias, leading us back to his cabin.

'Aren't you coming too?' I ask, as we take cover under his verandah.

He nods. 'Yes, but I have to finish revising the chapter of the book I'm working on first. I'll attend in the fullness of time.'

Chapter 10

Cheezels

Kane and I run in the pouring rain to the door of Cath's cabin. It's dark now and feels colder than ever.

As we get closer, we can hear music over the soaring wind and thunder. Sounds like some tragic eighties song. Given this is Cath's fiftieth, it tracks.

'Is it bad manners to turn up a few minutes before 6 pm?' I ask, checking my phone for the time. Still no signal.

'Who cares, I'm starving,' Kane says, and knocks on the ribbed glass door.

Maxine answers, swaying slightly, a full glass of white wine in her hand. 'Oh, it's the strangers! Come in boys, grab a drink.'

'Great,' says Kane, as he walks inside confidently, with me following. Maxine's eyes are glued to him as he strides past.

'Nice arse,' she giggles. So weird. She's probably the same age as his mum! Over Maxine's shoulder I can see Shell standing in the kitchen with Greta, helping her sort food into bowls. She winces at Maxine's comment.

The cabin is much larger than ours. There's an open kitchen and living area and three doors, which must lead to two bedrooms and a bathroom. The kitchen is fairly modern compared to ours and appears to be freshly painted. Coloured homemade streamers are hanging off the cupboards and across the curtain rails above the sink. The living room is almost twice the size of ours, with two grey three-seater couches facing each other, covered in a variety of cushions, all different shades of green. Between them is a highly polished wooden coffee table with interesting grain, partly covered by a meat and cheese platter and several bowls of chips. There's also a high-backed chair sitting in the corner, alongside a tall bookcase and a freestanding lamp.

On the walls are a few abstract paintings, in shades of grey and green too, as if chosen to match the furniture. There's a flatscreen TV with party lights around its edges. I can see a gaming console tucked away in the cabinet below, next to what I guess is a satellite box that they must use for phone and internet.

It's super odd to be in the middle of a room full of strangers, in the middle of a storm, in the middle of nowhere.

I hand over my box of Cheezels to Shell who promptly dumps the packet out into a bowl. She then slides a Cheezel on each of her fingers and comes at me like a tiger, her signature move. I smile and brush her away.

Cath is standing in the middle of the room, holding a stubby of beer, wearing a garishly bright green dress. She has a paper crown on her head, the type you get in a Christmas cracker. There is actually something regal about her, despite her getup. Straight back, strong features, and eyes that seem to take in everything. She doesn't look silly wearing a paper hat, especially compared to Greta, whose crown sits askew on her head, making her look off kilter.

I look for Nash and see Mr Scowlface poking his head out his bedroom door. He grabs a beer then dashes back in, not making eye contact with anyone.

I want to ask them all if they know what Walker was talking about earlier, but I chicken out. It feels wrong to put them on the spot right away, given that they have let us stay here and even invited us to this party.

The three of us sit together on the couch and watch the others. It's like watching a documentary. The Circle creatures in their natural habitat. Their rituals and mannerisms are really on show tonight. Cath is working hard to keep people talking, walking around offering food, engaging with everyone. Hostess and leader rolled into one.

Greta follows Cath about like a child, her fist full of chips. Maxine is dancing slinkily to the music, running her hands through her raccoon hair. Nash is holed up in his room.

Around 6.30, Tobias arrives. He has a puzzled look on his face, and I wonder what's on his mind. He hangs his black jacket by the door with the others, opens the bottle of red wine that he has brought with him, and pours himself a glass. He mutters a hello to everyone then moves to the armchair in the corner, taking a book out of his tweed jacket pocket. He seems to have deliberately distanced himself from everyone else. The chair he is sitting in is in shadows but there's just enough light to see that he's watching us carefully. Dressed quite formally, he looks so out of place with this community.

'What are you reading?' I ask, for no good reason except I realise that while I've been staring at him, he's been staring back at me.

He shows me the cover: *Australian Stone Circle Myths and Stories.*

'Good read?' asks Kane, smiling innocently.

'Yes, actually,' he responds dryly, pointing to his name as author on the cover. 'This is what I stayed back to work on earlier. I'm revising it to include our circle here.'

'How many do we have in Australia?'

'Australia has a few stone circles, but not many. That's why I'm doing a megalithic and anthropological significance analysis of this circle, as they are quite rare.'

I have no idea what that means. 'Are any of the ones we have as big as Stonehenge?'

He smiles crookedly.

'Not really. Stonehenge is a complex circle of standing stones, one of the big five in the British Isles. Our stones aren't bluestone or sandstone like Stonehenge.'

Cath comes over to us, holding out the bowl of chips. 'It wasn't until I bought this land and cleared some of the severely overgrown bushland behind the cabins that it was even uncovered.'

I take a handful of chips and scoff them down. I didn't realise how hungry I was till just now.

'It's special,' says a voice behind me. Greta comes up behind Cath. 'We've gotta protect it.'

'From Walker?' I ask.

'From everyone.'

Tobias puts his book down and taps it with his hand vigorously. 'Once I get it classified as culturally significant, we can preserve it and stop Walker or anyone from turning it into a tourist attraction.'

Greta nods. 'Walker keeps offering Cath more money, but she'd never sell – would you?' she says, glancing at Cath.

'Of course not,' Cath replies instantly. Her eyes don't meet Greta's, her expression at odds with her answer.

I hear some high-pitched giggling and see Maxine over on the other side of the room, seemingly flirting with Kane. He's not hating her attention. Her impressive cleavage is barely contained in the low-cut leopard top she's wearing.

Maybe he's got a thing for older women now? Her long fingernails seem to caress his bicep now and then, as he talks to her. Just a touch, but enough. I mean, he's nineteen and she's pushing forty, so it's not illegal, just very creepy.

Despite the cold, Kane's still in just a T-shirt, one of those ones where the arms are too tight and sit above his biceps. I mean, if I looked like him, I'd be shameless too, I guess. But I feel like what he does on socials and what he is in real life are starting to blur lately. To be fair though, my socials are full of books and *Doctor Who* clips, so who I am to judge him?

He's describing his gym routine to Maxine, which she seems to find more interesting than I ever do. She's bright eyed and perky as he bangs on about it. He's showing her some pictures on his phone, probably the ones that he calls 'progress shots' but I think are just an excuse for him to flex and pose without a shirt. Still, he's got a really big social media following, so I guess it's working.

Shell stands next to me, watching their interaction and rolling her eyes. 'She's even tossing her hair like she's a high school mean girl,' she mutters.

At one point, Maxine takes a hanky from her cleavage, dabs at her brow, and puts it away neatly.

'What else have you got hidden there?' jokes Kane. She giggles again and mock slaps his wrist, which accidentally knocks the chips out of his hand. When he reaches down to pick them up, I see her perky smile fall away. She looks tired. Not sure if it's tired in general or tired from feigning interest in Kane's conversation. Either way, it's a dramatic change and she looks like she's bearing the weight of the world. She looks at her watch and I wonder if she wants to be out of here. Is her behaviour all a facade?

Shell taps me on the shoulder. 'I'm just going out for a quick smoke.'

'You'll freeze! Aren't you trying to quit?' I say.

'Maybe, but it's been a long day,' she says. She takes a smoke from her packet, finds her lighter, then braces herself as she opens the door. Everyone turns around as the wind blasts suddenly through the room. She quickly shuts the door behind her.

I'm just about to return to my conversation with Tobias when

Greta comes out of the kitchen with a birthday cake and a large pearl-handled cake knife. Maxine takes a red BBQ lighter off the kitchen bench and lights the candles.

'Happy birthda—' she starts to sing, when suddenly the door flies open again. Shell is standing in the doorway, white as a ghost, her unlit smoke dangling out of the corner of her mouth.

'*Fire!*'

'No need to be rude, I'm not that old,' laughs Cath.

Shell shakes her head, pointing behind her. 'No, seriously, there's a fire on the lake!'

Chapter 11

Houseboat

Everyone stares at her. Cath looks at her with disdain, like Shell's a child vying for attention. Greta looks confused and wobbles on her feet. It looks like she's going to drop the cake, but Cath quickly takes it from her hands and puts it down on the coffee table. Maxine stops flirting with Kane, and Tobias stands up and walks over to Shell at the front door, concerned.

'Hello? There's a fire down by the lake. Didn't you all hear me? I can just see it through the storm.'

Cath frowns. 'How could there be a fire in the middle of a storm this bad?'

Shell's agitated now and gestures behind her. 'Why would I make this up? Come and see for yourself.'

Everyone moves toward the doorway. With the storm and cutting wind, it's hard to see clearly, but there's definitely something on fire out there. And it seems to be by the jetty, where we saw that lone houseboat moored earlier.

Cath walks out onto the verandah to get a closer look, peering out into the night. 'Lucky no one's down there now. Everyone moved to town to avoid the worst of this storm.'

'There was still one houseboat left there when we drove up earlier,' Shell says.

'I better call the firies,' Cath says. She grabs her phone out of her pocket, then stops. 'Bugger, I forgot there's no signal.'

Tobias's voice comes from behind me. 'We should go down and see if we can put it out. It might spread to the jetty and even around to Vince's shop.'

'In this storm? Are you mad?' says Maxine. Her voice is a bit louder than everyone else's. She seems drunk, holding onto the doorframe with white knuckles.

Cath turns back to us, her face halfway between panic and calm. She seems to steel herself before she speaks. I can see why she is the leader here. 'Well, I'm going to go down there and see if we can put it out somehow. I don't expect you all to come, but I could do with some help.'

'I'll come with you,' Shell says, putting up her hand like we're being picked for a job at school.

'Me too,' I say. I don't want to go but I know it's the right thing to do. Shell is basically my moral compass. True north with combat boots.

'We'll need the fire extinguisher. Nash . . .' Cath looks around her, puzzled. 'Where's Nash?'

No one seems to know where he is. Cath heads back into the cabin and knocks on one of the bedroom doors, calling out his name.

'He's not here!' she says, panic in her voice. 'Maybe he saw the fire and went to take a look? Surely he didn't . . .'

She stumbles, and Tobias takes her hand. 'Let's all go and look for him and see what can be done about the fire.'

Greta whimpers. 'No. Fire and lightning scare me.'

Cath snaps back into action. 'You don't have to come. Maxine will look after you.'

Maxine nods, grabbing a fire extinguisher from out of the cupboard under the kitchen sink and handing it to Cath.

'I'm not sure it will work in this rain. Maybe we should get one of the bigger ones from the garage?' says Cath.

Tobias shakes his head. 'Possibly. But let's just see what we are dealing with first.'

Grabbing our jackets and umbrellas, Cath, Tobias, and the three of us walk out into the storm, heading down the hill toward the lake. We have to put our umbrellas in front of us like shields to protect ourselves from the horizontal rain.

'Naaaash!' Cath yells, over and over. We all start calling out his name too. Nothing. The wind is so strong, it feels like the words are just thrown back in our faces, almost mocking us.

'Why are *we* going?' asks Kane.

'Because it's the right thing to do. And they are putting us up,' replies Shell abruptly.

I hate being this wet and cold. My canvas runners and socks are soaked already.

'I see him! We need to go sideways here,' Cath yells over the wind, pointing to another trail I can barely see with the relentless rain coming at us. Each drop feels like a tiny needle hitting me in the face.

Shell and I look at each other, worried. There is something ominous about the squelching water around our feet now, like the storm is flooding the ground. How far up will the water reach?

As we get closer to the edge of the lake, it's clear that the houseboat that we saw earlier is what's burning. The glass walls have cracked, the hull is blackened and there's a terrible chemical smell. The whole vessel is rocking in the wind, despite being tethered by rope to the jetty's metal fence rails.

'Nash!' shouts Cath, with relief this time. We can just make him out. He's on the jetty, his shape lit up by the fire, but he's just standing there, staring, not moving.

It seems like the fire is almost out, the flames getting smaller by the second. There's steam rising around it, fogging the air.

'How can the houseboat be on fire in all this rain?' I ask Shell. 'And why is it steaming?'

Shell shouts over the wind. 'Fire needs oxygen to burn, so maybe the rain isn't falling heavily enough to put it out.' As usual, she says things with such authority that even if it were total crap, it still sounds convincing.

'How much heavier could it be?' Kane yells.

On the jetty, Nash seems to be pointing to something. Cath turns back to Tobias, ashen-faced, before bolting along the wooden jetty, stumbling a little on the wet boards as she goes.

'Careful, Cath,' yells Tobias as he follows her.

Suddenly Cath screams loudly enough to drown out the storm. She falls to her knees by what looks to be a body splayed out on the jetty, arms askew, one foot stuck in the jetty's fence rail.

I feel sick.

'*He's dead!*' Cath wails, like a wounded animal.

Shell and I hold each other. Kane gulps.

All I can focus on is the huge watch on the body's wrist.

Chapter 12

Body

The dead body has to be Simon Walker.

I puke. Thanks to the rain and wind, a splash of it blows back in my face, which is completely gross. Shell robotically wipes my face with her sleeve without a second thought, as she makes gasping noises like a fish out of water. She's clearly in shock. Kane's frozen on my other side, saying 'Shit!' over and over.

Cath is crying, and Tobias is comforting her, patting her shoulder. Nash is still just staring at the blackened houseboat like he's a zombie. Bug-eyed, pale and drenched, with no umbrella.

'He's definitely dead?' Shell calls out to no one in particular.

I chance another look at the body, but have to look away immediately. I'm so shaken I feel the old urge rise back up in me sharply. My old cutting scars are calling me, offering something other than this to feel.

Tobias is talking to Cath. 'Yes. I checked his pulse. I think . . . it would have been quick . . .' he drifts off, then turns to Kane. 'Could you help me free his foot, please? I'm sorry to ask, but I can't do it on my own.'

Kane doesn't look thrilled by the request, muttering to himself as he edges down the jetty. He and Tobias carefully free Walker's foot from the rail, slowly lifting it up and twisting it slightly sideways to slip through the fence. Kane shudders as he touches his leg, but he keeps going. I forgot how good he is in an emergency.

We're all frozen, a sad audience to a disaster, staring helplessly at the body from under our wind-strained umbrellas. There's more steam than ever, but the flames have subsided. The rain has finally won, but too late for Walker.

Nash seems to suddenly jolt back into the real world when the last flame ebbs out, like someone has hit play on a paused film. He stumbles and looks around wildly, like he doesn't remember how he got here. *What is going through his head?*

Tobias creeps to the edge of the jetty.

'What are you doing?' Cath shouts.

'Just checking no one else is here,' he calls back.

'Be careful,' she replies. 'Take this.'

He takes the fire extinguisher that she brought with her and gingerly steps onto the houseboat, pulling his jacket sleeves over his hand as he grips the rails. He shoots bolts of foam ahead of him, squelching any remaining flames, though the rain spreads half the foam away as fast as he sprays it. Then he is gone inside the houseboat and I can't see him anymore.

After a minute he reappears, gingerly moving to the side of the houseboat. Just before he steps out, I think I can see him putting something in his pocket before he braces himself on the railing and carefully climbs back onto the jetty. He walks over to a wild-eyed Cath, who is still crouched beside Walker's body.

'We can't just leave him here,' I hear Cath yell over the wind.

Tobias turns to us. 'You kids go back and take Nash with you before you all catch your death . . .' he catches himself too late. 'Tell the others what has happened and we will be along soon. We just need to sort things out here first,' he says, gesturing to Walker's body.

It's totally right to get Walker – Walker's body, that is – out of the storm, but despite everything, I keep thinking that the police wouldn't like him messing with a scene like this.

I nudge Nash, but he doesn't move. I try again, this time almost pushing him forward.

The trip back from the houseboat is a blur. Literally. We can't see a thing in the storm. The rain keeps coming so it is even harder getting back to Cath's cabin. And when we do get there, Maxine and Greta are eager to know what has happened. We all look at one another, cold and wet and shivering, not sure where to begin.

I feel so strange. I can't think of what to say, what to tell them. Where do you start?

'That bloke Walker's houseboat was on fire,' Kane says to them, his voice shaking.

Maxine grabs some towels from Cath's linen cupboard and hands one to each of us. 'Oh no, it's a nice houseboat. Was it burnt badly?' she asks. She rubs her hands together anxiously.

'It looks pretty bad,' I say, 'but it's out now.'

'How does fire happen in the rain?' Greta asks. It's a good question.

Shell and I give each other a look. 'We don't know. But ... someone was hurt,' she says softly.

Greta gasps. 'Who? Not Cath?' She looks panicked.

Shell shakes her head, takes a breath. 'When we got down to the jetty, there was a burnt body.'

Greta and Maxine grab each other's hands. Nash is still looking shellshocked.

'A body? Are you saying ... do you mean someone ... died? Who?' Maxine stutters.

Nash suddenly finds his voice. 'Walker is dead.'

They both look horrified. Greta sobs and runs into the bathroom. There is the sound of vomiting, then the flush of a toilet.

Maxine picks up her wine from the bench and takes a swig. 'Jesus.' She's as white as a ghost and looks sick too. 'Are you sure?' she asks, taking another gulp.

'Yes,' Nash replies, his voice distant, like he's fading out of reality.

Maxine slumps into a chair like a broken doll. Her reaction is stronger than I expected, but I guess I don't really know her at all. 'I mean, I didn't like him, but that's awful,' she says tearily.

Greta comes back from the bathroom, wiping her mouth on a hand towel, her big glasses now in her hand. 'Why would he be on the houseboat? We saw him drive to town.'

'What do you mean?' I say.

'He lives in the Walliss township and rarely uses that houseboat,' Maxine explains, nails tapping on her wineglass.

'Maybe the water was too high near the boom gate and he couldn't get through,' Kane suggests quietly. 'I didn't see his car anywhere. He might have gone to the houseboat to sit it out?'

Nobody has anything else to say. Silently, we take off our wet jackets and keep drying ourselves with the towels we've been given.

'Oh God,' says Maxine suddenly. 'Where are Cath and Tobias? Are they doing something with . . . um . . . his body?'

I nod. 'I think so. They didn't want to just leave him there out in the storm.'

Greta looks horrified and starts crying properly. 'They won't actually bring it into *this* cabin, will they?' she asks between sobs.

Shell shakes her head. 'I don't know. I don't think so.'

Nash visibly shudders. 'Better not.'

Maxine shakes her head and stands up. 'What am I like? Here we are interrogating you when you kids have just had a traumatic experience. Give me those wet towels and sit down.' She goes into the kitchen, returning with the chips from the party and glasses of orange juice.

'Sugar for shock, plus a dash of voddy for your nerves.'

'It's not a party anymore, Maxine,' whispers Greta.

We sit in silence, sipping our too-strong drinks. Suddenly Cath and Tobias rush through the door, slamming it shut against the wind behind them.

'We told them what happened,' Nash says.

'Yes, I thought as much.' She walks over to Greta and puts her arm around her heaving shoulders. It's a very maternal gesture, and Greta seems to settle a little with her touch. I notice Nash's lip curls in disgust.

Tobias wipes his face and turns away, clearly drying his eye patch. He turns back and sees me looking. I feel guilty.

'Um . . . where's Walker?'

'We took him to my cabin. He's in my spare bedroom, for now. We can call the police once we can get a signal from the satellite.'

He throws the towel he's using to the floor and takes off his jacket. Maxine hands him a glass of the red wine he had earlier and he virtually downs it in one gulp. Nash wordlessly passes Cath a knitted jumper and moves to the edge of the room. His eyes are focused now but he's still white as a ghost.

'How did this happen?' Cath asks, gesturing for Tobias to sit down on the couch. 'How does a houseboat suddenly catch fire in weather like this?'

Tobias rubs his good eye. 'I didn't say anything at the time, but coming over tonight, I thought I heard something, a strange booming noise. I assumed it was thunder or just the wind howling or a tree being blown over, but now . . .' his voice trails off.

Cath looks up at him. 'You think his engine blew or something?'

He nods. 'Possibly.'

'Do boats catch fire often?' I ask.

'No,' Cath says. Her brow is furrowed and her fingers are plucking at a thread on her jumper.

I walk over to the window and pull back the curtain. Touching the glass, I can almost feel the wind pushing back at me. There's no sign that the storm will stop any time soon.

I'm still stuck on the image of a houseboat on fire in the middle of a big storm. It was such a horrible, vivid sight, but at the same time undeniably striking. Vibrant flames in a brutal storm. Walker was right, the storm was biblical in a way. Like two parts of nature that can't coexist, somehow doing an impossible dance together on the water.

Tobias stands in the middle of the room. 'We have all had a terrible shock tonight. I think we should all return to our cabins and try and get some sleep. We cannot do anything more for Walker until we have phone reception and can reach the police, which I suspect will not be until the morning at least.'

Everyone seems to agree and we all start to make our way back to our cabins. Greta has calmed down but is still sniffling quietly, while Maxine struggles to put on her jacket with her hands shaking. Cath looks exhausted as she fusses over Nash, who has gone silent again. Tobias mainly looks concerned as he ushers people out the door.

As for us, we stare at each other, entirely overwhelmed.

Chapter 13

Bag

We stumble back up to our cabin, even though it feels like two steps forward, one step back, as the rain continues to barrage us, stinging my face. Kane gets there first of course, and shoves some of the sandbags out of the way before holding the door open for us. We pull the sandbags back up behind us and slam the door shut, sealing the storm outside.

We shed our jackets and try to dry ourselves off again. In the bathroom I scrub my teeth to get the taste of puke and vodka out of my mouth. Wrapped in towels, we all settle in on the couch and try to take stock of what just happened.

I can't stop seeing Walker's body in my head, all burnt like that. It was horrible.

I feel really shaky and the scars on my stomach are starting to itch like never before. I haven't cut myself this year at all, but it's not like the temptation hasn't been there. It's times like this when everything is spinning out of hand that I want to take back control and feel that sweet pain, that release. I have my Swiss Army Knife in my bag. I'll have to wait until the others have gone to bed. But if Kane's in here and Shell's in the bedroom with me, then I'll have to sneak into the bathroom . . .

What am I thinking? I know that I have to break out of this thought cycle. My psych says I'm drawn to self-harm because it's my way of shifting my feelings from my head to my body. Whenever this feeling comes over me, I have to take very deep breaths and think of something positive and focus on that. I breathe in … then out … then in … then out. I hold onto the couch arm firmly, keeping grounded.

'What you thinking about?' Shell asks as she lights up a smoke. When we both look at her, she says, 'C'mon, normally I'd go outside, but I'm not going back out in that shitshow.' She walks to the kitchen and comes back with a saucer to use as an ashtray.

'Do you guys think it was deliberate?' I ask.

'Yes,' says Shell. 'No,' says Kane – at the exactly the same time.

They do a double take, looking at one another.

'If Tobias really heard an explosion, then yes,' Shell says.

'But how?' asks Kane. 'How did someone even get in here and blow up the houseboat in a storm like this and get out again?'

I try to think how a detective would approach this situation. 'If I was a cop—'

Kane interrupts. 'Which you're not.'

I roll my eyes. '*Okay,* sure. But if I were, the first thing I would do is secure the crime scene to protect the evidence. Then I would get forensics to look at the body and the scene as a whole. If I was a detective dealing with the storm and the rain, I'd be super annoyed to find out that Tobias had gone onto the houseboat, and then that he and Cath moved the body. The whole crime scene is stuffed already.'

I sit up a bit straighter, realising that talking this through is calming me down somehow. 'The next thing I'd do is look at the houseboat to determine if this was deliberate or not. If it looked deliberate, I'd look at everyone's motives and opportunity.'

Shell looks thoughtful as she grinds her smoke out in the saucer. 'With this storm, the road by the boom gate is probably flooded now. It's the only way in or out, so there's no way anyone else could have gotten in. More likely they were already here.'

I nod. 'Yes. Plus, we watched as Walker literally stood there and told everyone he knew all their secrets and he was going to take their home away and exploit their stone circle. That's pretty clear motive to want to get back at him, or even get rid of him.'

Shell clasps her hands together. 'Exactly, it *must* be one of them. Unless someone else is hidden here that we don't know about? Isn't there an empty cabin?'

Kane shakes his head as he undoes his boots. 'Hang on, we don't actually know what happened. It could have been an accident.'

He's got a point, but so do we. 'I just feel like it's too much of a coincidence that he basically threatened everyone this afternoon and winds up dead a few hours later.'

Kane sighs. 'Okay, if it's one of the others, then who? Greta's scared of her own shadow. Maxine is a drunk. Tobias is a maybe, though he vibes too much as "posh professor" to do something like this. Cath? She's pretty tough. And Nash is a wildcard. I mean, we did find him staring at the fire and the body in some kind of trance.'

'Maybe he was in shock?' I say. I feel like I'm in shock myself. I can't stop thinking about Walker's body. I hate the thought that he's just a cabin away. The whole thing gives me the creeps. I start shuddering again.

Shell looks at me. 'Are you okay?'

I nod but it's not true. My hands are sweating and shaking, and my head is spinning.

'This is nuts,' says Kane. 'We came here looking for your birth mother, Goose. We didn't expect to find a dead body.'

Yes, Jane. I'd almost forgotten why we were here.

'I might go to bed,' I say. I do feel like crap. My head is all over the place. Plus, if Shell stays up for a while, I might get a chance to do a small cut.

'Me too,' Shell says.

Damn. She gets up and goes into the bedroom.

'Are you okay Goose?' Kane asks. *'Really?'*

I shake my head. 'Not really, but I probably just need a good night's sleep.'

He gives me the thumbs up. 'Hey, can you get me another towel?' he asks.

'Seeing you've lost the power to walk, sure,' I joke weakly. When I come back and hand it to him he has a strange look on his face.

'What's up?' I ask. 'Are *you* okay?'

'Yup, all good,' he replies.

What's he up to? Whatever, I'm too tired to think about it. I grab my bag and head to the bedroom. Shell's already in bed and looks like she's out to it. Just as I'm about to climb in, I realise I need the bathroom.

Stepping quietly out of the bedroom, I see Kane in the darkened kitchen. He's taking all of the knives out of the drawers and putting them in his sports bag. Shit, he really does know me. I feel touched that he cares this much, but I also know how much better I'll feel if I can cut. Anyway, I have my Swiss Army Knife in my bag, so I'm good to go.

He turns out the light. It's not long before he seems to settle in to sleep, pulling an old blanket over himself. I wait till he's stopped shuffling around on the couch and his breathing changes before I start rummaging in my bag, looking for my Swiss Army Knife, figuring I can sneak past Kane and cut in the bathroom. I pull all of my stuff out and look in every corner of the empty bag, but it's not there. I absolutely packed it.

Suddenly I remember how weirdly Kane was acting earlier. I bet he went through my bag when I was in the bathroom getting him that extra towel! I'm furious, but exhaustion takes over. Getting into bed, the anger fades and I'm left with this overwhelming sense of luck having such good friends.

Chapter 14

Gizmo

The next day I wake up unsure where I am. The musty smell of the bedclothes and the murky light shining through the window are unfamiliar. Everything comes rushing back all at once: the cabin, the houseboat, the fire . . . the body. How did we go from looking for my mother to finding a dead body on the jetty? How did I even manage to sleep? Is exhaustion a side effect of shock?

Shell isn't on her side of the bed so she must be up already. I scratch at my scars, so glad that I didn't fall back into old habits last night, even though I'm still kind of annoyed that Kane went through my stuff. I've made good progress with my psych and I haven't cut for ages. Truthfully, I haven't felt that urge in a long time. This place has really thrown me off . . . Mum was right about this being a bad idea, but it's too late now.

I get dressed and go into the lounge room where Shell and Kane are sitting on the couch. They're both already dressed and looking awkward in one another's company, not talking, scrolling on their phones.

'Have we got reception back?' I ask, reaching for my phone on the kitchen bench.

Kane shakes his head. 'Nup, just going through pics I took yesterday.'

'I've been making a timeline of last night in Notes,' adds Shell, holding up her phone to me. 'Glad you had a sleep in.'

Kane stands up and stretches. 'I feel like I didn't sleep at all. And now I'm starving. We have no food up here. Should we go back down to Cath's place and see if we can scam some brekky?'

I sit down next to Shell and she shows me the timeline she's been working on.

Timeline

3.15 pm we arrive

3.30 pm Walker arrives

3.45 pm Walker leaves

4.00 pm sandbagging

4.45 pm we finish sandbagging and set up cabin six

5.30 pm Shell goes to cabin one, Greta already there. Gus and Kane go to cabin five to see Tobias. Cath is in garden, Nash in room? Maxine getting ready

5.45 pm sunset

5.50 pm Maxine arrives at cabin one

5.55 pm Gus and Kane leave cabin five and arrive at cabin one

6.25 pm Tobias hears boom. Explosion?

6.30 pm Tobias arrives at cabin one

6.45 pm Shell sees the fire

'This is great, really thorough. And you refer to yourself in the third person. Very objective.'

She laughs a little.

'Come and have a look at this, Kane,' I say.

'Can't we find some brekky first?' he says, tapping his foot impatiently.

'A man is dead,' says Shell, 'and all you can think of is food?'

'It's not our fault he's dead,' says Kane pragmatically.

'Well, it's not his fault either,' replies Shell.

Something dawns on me. 'It kinda is though.'

'What do you mean?' asks Shell, frowning at me.

'It's part of police training. To know who the killer is, you need to know the victim. If you think about it, Walker was pretty awful. I mean, he wanted to buy this land, which would leave everyone here homeless, and he wanted to exploit the circle as well. You saw how everyone reacted to him yesterday, and how he threatened to reveal everyone's secrets. They all had a reason to hate him. Any one of them could have hated him enough to blow up the houseboat.'

'You could be right,' agrees Kane. 'But they all thought he went back to town, like we did. How would one of them even know he was still here? Could it have been an accident? Or an insurance job gone wrong or something? You two are jumping to the conclusion it was murder, but we don't know that.'

'That's true,' I say. 'But like I said last night, he really set himself up for something yesterday. To come at everyone as aggressively as he did, and then suddenly wind up dead in suspicious circumstances . . . that tracks like murder to me.'

'Hold on. Wanting to make money and being ignorant of the cultural importance of the stones makes him a dick, sure, but it doesn't mean he deserved to be murdered!' counters Shell.

'No, I didn't say he *deserved* it, just that he pissed someone off with his actions enough to do him in,' I reply. 'He may have *contributed* to it . . .'

Shell shakes her head. 'No matter what kind of person he was, that's victim blaming.'

'I'm trying to think like a cop—'

'If a woman gets attacked by a man and she's wearing a short skirt, did she *contribute* to her attack?'

'No!'

'It's the same thing, Gus.'

'It's . . . no, you're right. Sorry, I got carried away.'

'Well, my vote is accident still,' says Kane. 'And breakfast.'

I go to the side window and look out at the stones. The rain has settled down, but it's misty up there, and the stone circle looks just as spooky in the morning light as it did yesterday. I wonder how old they are, and who put them there, and why.

'Hey, check out the circle,' I call out to the others. They both come and have a look. We stand there at the window for a while, just looking. It's mesmerising.

Suddenly my stomach rumbles loudly enough to break the silence.

Kane elbows me, grinning, and goes to grab our jackets. 'C'mon, let's go to Cath's.'

We shrug on our damp jackets and brace ourselves for the rain and the cold. Opening the door, we work quickly to push the sandbags away and then back into place. Cath's cabin is only about twenty metres away but we are trudging through dirty paths that are just mud. Kane has leather hi-tops on, and Shell has big combat boots. They're both faring better than me. My canvas runners are still wet from last night. I can't remember the last time my toes felt warm.

We're just shaking ourselves dry under the verandah at cabin one when Cath opens the door and waves us in, back in her green jumper and jeans. She doesn't look that happy to see us.

'I wondered when you lot would turn up,' she says in a resigned voice. 'Put your jackets here with the others.'

Inside, it's complete déjà vu – everyone else is back here as well, as if they never left the party. The only difference is their clothes. At least they have dry things to change into.

We try to find somewhere to sit down. No one is talking and the silence is overwhelming. Everyone is looking at us suspiciously, like we're strangers walking into a small town's only pub in a horror film. I can tell by the way Shell has changed her posture, all tall and strong, as if ready to fight, that she can feel the hostility too. Kane, however, seems oblivious.

Cath looks us up and down. 'Well, seems like you're stuck here for now.'

She gives us another look before moving into the kitchen. Moments later she comes out with five or six pieces of toast on a plate.

'It feels heartless to eat after what happened last night, but it's only toast, so . . .'

I've never really thought about what the protocol is for food after a death.

She puts the plate down, then brings out some smaller plates, some margarine, some Vegemite and a jar of jam.

'Oh, I forgot the knives,' she says, going back to the kitchen.

We can use the ones in Kane's bag, I think to myself with a snort.

Greta still looks upset. 'I can't believe what's happened,' she says. Her feet seem to be shaking in her boots.

Maxine stares into space. 'We saw him drive off toward town.'

'Yeah, but maybe the road was already flooding by then. He probably tried to drive through the water and got stuck, so he left the car on the path and legged it back to the boat for cover,' says Kane.

'Who asked you?' snarls Nash from the corner of the room, not looking up from his Nintendo Switch.

Kane goes to reply but I tap him on the arm and shake my head. He frowns at me, but says nothing.

'But why go to the houseboat, why not come here?' Maxine says, to no one in particular.

Cath looks at her with surprise as she sets some knives down on the coffee table. 'Really, after everything that was said, would you come back here?'

'He was nasty to us,' protests Greta.

'Yes, and some of us were nasty back,' Cath says, one eyebrow arched as she looks at Tobias and then Nash.

'Fine, I'm sorry I threw sand at him or whatever,' sighs Nash.

Tobias sits up. 'Well, I do not regret what I said. It was the truth. I am sorry he is dead, but he was not a good person. He was enjoying taunting us yesterday.'

'He was just trying to do business, using whatever tactic he needed to get what he wanted,' says Cath, turning to head back to the kitchen. 'I used to be the same.'

She rustles around in the kitchen, clinking cups together and flicking the kettle on. 'Tea or coffee for you three? No fancy Melbourne coffee here, just instant.'

'Tea,' we say in unison.

Maxine looks at us, her eyes narrowed in dark slits. 'We were a peaceful little community until you kids turned up, and now someone is dead.'

'It's just a coincidence!' Kane snaps, his voice louder than usual.

'Exactly,' I say quickly, surprised at his tone. *Why is he so angry?*

'But it isn't a coincidence, is it?' Tobias says evenly, standing up to stretch his legs. 'Someone sent you here looking for your mother.'

'Yes, *someone* told us to come,' I say. 'So we're not here by accident. But none of you know Jane, right?'

Everyone goes silent once again. The rain lashes against the cabin in waves, the noise of water going in gutters and downpipes. Nash's fingers click on his Nintendo. Greta's laces are slapping against her shoes as she fidgets nervously.

'We've been thinking about what happened to Simon all morning,' Shell says, rubbing the bridge of her nose, always a sign that she's onto something. 'When did all this happen? I saw the fire at maybe 6.45, but when do we think it actually started?'

Cath barks from the kitchen. 'What gives you the right to be asking questions? You said yourself you have no connection to this, so butt out.'

Greta nods fervently.

'Once we get a mobile signal again, we can contact the police and they'll figure out how this awful accident happened,' Maxine says, crossing her arms.

'I'm not so sure it *was* an accident,' Tobias says quietly. He reaches into his pocket and pulls out a blackened object which he places on the coffee table in front of us. It looks like a chunk of melted metal, about the size of a mobile phone. Looking closer, I can see that it's actually a thin metal disc with a couple of twisted wires extending from it.

'I found this last night when I was checking that no one else was on the houseboat.'

I thought I saw him pocket something on his way out of the houseboat, but I'd forgotten all about it with everything else that was going on.

We all peer at it.

'What is it?' asks Maxine.

Tobias clears his throat. 'I believe it is a makeshift fire starter, but with no access to the internet, I cannot be sure.'

Greta leans in close to the gizmo, peering at it with a strange look on her face. Her glasses have slid halfway down her nose, and she looks like a nanna rather than a young woman. 'It's hard to say. It could be part of the engine?'

Tobias shakes his head no. 'My hypothesis is that this device points to the fire having been deliberately lit.'

Silence.

Cath makes a strange clicking noise with her tongue. I can't tell if it's disbelief or anger or something else. Maxine looks mortified, wringing her hands together to stop them shaking. Greta pushes her glasses back up her nose. And Nash is back staring into space again, his Switch dangling from his hand.

Shell stands up and starts to pace back and forth, her hands behind her back like a professor pacing in front of a class. 'But if it was deliberate, how did the person not get burnt alongside Walker?'

'I am not a mechanic, but I think you could possibly set this device to spark. It might take a little while for the vapour around the engine to catch light, which would give you time to get off the houseboat before anything happened.'

Greta frowns. 'That would be really hard to do.'

'Did the person who lit the fire know that Simon was on the houseboat?' Cath asks, gathering up cups and plates from the coffee table and taking them into the kitchen.

Tobias spreads his hands in an *I don't know* gesture.

Cath dumps the dirty dishes in the sink with a clatter before turning back to Tobias. 'But if they got away, why didn't Simon? I don't understand.'

Tobias shrugs. 'We did find him with his foot caught in the railing.'

No one speaks for a moment. Are they being hit by the realisation that the fire might have been deliberately lit? That whoever sabotaged the houseboat knew Walker was on board?

I watch as Shell walks from one side of the cabin to the other, my head moving like it's a tennis match. 'So, Tobias,' she says. 'You think you heard the explosion at around 6.25, right?'

He nods.

'Okay, so if the road was already flooding by then, it's possible that Walker couldn't get through the boom gate and decided to wait out the storm in his houseboat, which explains why he was trapped by the fire. But that leads to the next problem: if the entry gate was flooded, nobody else could get in.'

The energy in the room shifts. They all know what Shell means. The three of us have already considered this possibility, but I wonder if the others have. I look around, trying to gauge their reactions.

They all look at her and then each other, confusion and understanding and fear rippling through the room. There is an unnerving silence now. I wonder what they're all thinking. I wonder which one of them may have done this.

Tobias touches the tip of his cap in a gesture to Shell. 'Yes. I had the same thought. Whoever lit the fire is likely still here.'

Cath frowns. 'Really, Tobias? Someone could have hidden at the caravan park. Vince might not have noticed a straggler.'

Nash moves over to the couch and leans over behind Greta, lightly brushing his fingers on her shoulder and making her jump.

'Maybe the killer hid under your bed, Greta,' he snickers.

Greta pales. 'Don't!'

Cath rolls her eyes. 'Leave her alone.'

Then she turns to Tobias. 'Why don't you and I go and have a look around and check that someone else isn't hiding here?'

It's funny how they seem to be the mum and dad figures here. Tobias nods at Cath, standing and moving to the door to collect his jacket.

'And just leave us here?' asks Maxine. It sounds less like a question and more of a request. Like Greta, she looks quite relieved that she doesn't have to go out in the rain to check, just like last night.

'I think Tobias and I can handle this on our own,' says Cath, as she takes a few sets of keys from a row of hooks on the kitchen wall.

'Can we come?' I ask.

'Why?' asks Cath, frowning.

'We want to help,' I reply. *I want to snoop* would be more accurate.

Cath is about to say something when Tobias speaks instead. 'You can come, but we need to find you better shoes.'

My ruined sneakers seem to squelch in response. Yep, good idea.

Cath looks at Nash. 'Have you got any that he can borrow?'

Nash looks annoyed, but goes into his bedroom, emerging a minute later with a pair of dirty work boots. He hands them over and grins as their smell makes me grimace.

'Nice and ripe, mate,' he sniggers.

'Thanks,' I mutter as I take my shoes off and pull his boots on. They are a bit tight but they're better than what I have now, that's for sure. I've never worn anyone else's shoes before – it's a strange sensation. Oddly personal.

'Has anyone been able to get mobile signal yet?' asks Kane.

Cath shakes her head. 'We're all on satellite here. It's good most of the time, but bad storms do interfere with it. It'll come back soon.'

'When it does come back, we'll be able to contact the cops and they can get up here and sort out the . . . um . . . body, right?' Kane stammers.

'Argh,' moans Greta. Maxine puts an arm around her, rubbing her back in gentle circles.

'Nash, look after the girls for me – and be *nice*,' Cath says as we follow Tobias outside. I turn around just in time to see him give her the middle finger. He's standing behind Maxine and Greta, so no one else sees except me.

Chapter 15

Shed

We put our jackets back on and grab our umbrellas as we step out under the verandah.

'So, what's the plan?' I ask Tobias, bracing myself to be cold and wet again.

'We should do a methodical search of The Circle, and see if anyone is hiding here.'

'Like where? There's only the cabins, the generator shed and the garage. Someone would have noticed if there was someone in their cabin last night,' Shell says.

'Let's start with the generator shed and the garage then,' says Cath curtly.

Together we stride over to the generator shed. It gives off a diesel smell but the churning sound that it is making is somehow reassuring. When Tobias pulls open the door, all we can see is the bulky generator, some boxes of bits and pieces that I guess relate to it – spare parts, perhaps? – and a container with gardening tools.

Looking closer, it seems one box is full of actual machinery parts, but the other is just junk: a portable gas stove, a burnt out frypan, an alarm clock without a face, and an old toaster with a frayed cord. Why would anyone keep this rubbish?

Tobias points at the junk-filled boxes. 'Is that Maxine's clock? And my toaster? Clearly Greta is not as good at fixing things as she claims.'

Cath glares at him. 'We do use this as a bit of a dumping ground.'

She looks more closely at the container with the gardening implements. 'That's odd,' says Cath. 'The pitchfork is gone.'

Shell and I look at each other with a shudder. Pitchforks are slasher film staples.

'It'll just be left out in the garden somewhere,' says Tobias unconvincingly. 'Importantly, no one is here.'

At the larger shed on the other side of the property, Cath and Tobias hoist up the two garage doors with one big heave. There are four cars parked side-by-side, a bright orange but muddy quad bike, a dusty-looking table tennis table, and a lumpy old couch at one end.

'Wow,' says Shell.

'Awesome,' says Kane.

Even I am quite intrigued by the quad bike's impressive size: big handlebars, a seat like a ride-on mower, and monster wheels with tractor-like tyres. It's like an adult-sized toy.

Four cars. Presumably one each for Cath, Maxine, Greta and Tobias. There are two spaces empty, which must be parks allocated to John and our cabin.

Kane appraises the cars. 'SUV for Cath, pink Mazda for Maxine, old Corolla for Greta, Volvo for the professor, and quad bike for Nash.'

Tobias taps his head again, this time to Kane. 'Well done, Sherlock.'

Kane grins and takes his moment.

Shell gestures at the far wall, where several fire extinguishers are hung. 'Why are these fire extinguishers here? Shouldn't they be in the cabins?'

Cath gives her a withering look. 'We have them in the cabins too. These are for emergencies.'

Shell holds her gaze. Cath breaks first.

'Let's check inside the cars,' Tobias says. We move quietly around the shed, checking a vehicle each. I think of all the TV shows I've seen where someone was hiding in the backseat of a car, waiting to attack the driver from behind. Creepy.

The back seat of the Volvo is empty and spotless. That tracks for Tobias.

Cath calls out from the other end of the shed. 'Nobody here.'

Kane gives a thumbs up, and Shell shakes her head. Tobias shrugs; we all agree that there's no one hiding here.

Our cabin is the nearest to the garage so it's next.

'No one could have hidden here, not with three of us using every room,' Shell says as we open the door.

'Yes, but it's still worth having a look,' Tobias says over the wind.

Inside is a mess. Our stuff is spread out everywhere and I feel like Cath and Tobias want to comment, like parents who have been away for the weekend and come back to find the house in disarray. Shell starts to tidy up a little as she talks, suddenly channelling her mother.

'There's nowhere for anyone to hide here,' she says as she kicks Kane's bag under the couch.

'How come our cabin is empty?' I ask Cath, while Tobias inspects the bedroom and bathroom. I can hear him opening the wardrobe. *Seriously?* As if someone would be hiding in there.

'It's been vacant for some time now. While I could do with the money, I won't rent it out to just anyone. They have to be a good fit for our little community here.' As she speaks, I see that there's genuine care on her face. Her eyes shine with obvious pride in what she has built here. But how far would she go to protect her community if it was under threat?

'This cabin is clear,' Tobias announces as he returns to the living area. It's strange but I feel relieved, even though I knew he wouldn't find anyone in here.

Back out into the rain we go again, this time to Tobias's cabin.

Its layout is similar to ours, but a bit wider and with a second bedroom. Once inside, I have to stop and look at that creepy painting again. Like last time, I find myself drawn into it, hypnotised. The hues on the distorted stones are quite unsettling. When I blink, I swear it changes colour. *How?*

We walk through Tobias's main bedroom, which is also bare and tidy, but a bit musty. There's only a few items hanging in his wardrobe and he has a suitcase leaning against the wall. I guess he isn't really planning to be here long-term, unlike the others. He's only a visiting academic.

'There's no mirror,' Shell whispers to me. It makes a kind of sense, I guess. I wonder if he hates looking at his eye the way I hate looking at my body?

'Is Simon in there?' I ask him, looking tentatively at the second bedroom door.

Tobias nods. 'Yes. I suggest we leave him in peace.'

Cath looks upset as she stares at the closed door. But there's also a layer of something else I can't quite figure out. Fear? Guilt?

It feels so strange to be moving about in here, with Walker just in the other room. I start to shiver. Shell and Kane are both staring at the door too. It's hard to ignore that he's in there. How can Tobias stand it? Someone he knew, but didn't like, was burnt to death and is now in his spare room. He must have nerves of steel. If it was me, I would be afraid Walker's ghost would visit me in the night.

Part of me thinks that we should investigate the second bedroom, just to be sure no one's there. But would a killer really hide in the room with the body of the person they killed? Plus the thought of going in there, and what I might see, makes me feel nauseous. I shake my head and try to focus on literally anything else.

Just like Tobias himself, his home is hard to read. He seems so controlled most of the time, but then I remember him launching into Walker yesterday. He clearly has a temper. I wonder how far he would go if he was really provoked?

Next up is Greta's cabin. Waiting on the verandah while Cath rifles through her collection of keys, I try to picture what Greta's space will look like. I'm expecting it to be really kooky, and it is, but in an unexpected way. Cath steps through first as the key finally clicks in the lock, and we file in after her. This cabin has the same basic layout and bland furniture as ours, but it's actually like a Funko Pop shop, with dolls everywhere, their big square heads and saucer-like eyes staring out from above small bodies, through the plastic windows in their unopened boxes. There's a heap stacked up against one wall, neatly, almost to the ceiling. A wall of watchers. Spooky.

Where does she get all the money for these? It makes me wonder how any of these people survive. I mean, do any of them work? I guess Tobias does if he's an academic, but what about the others? How do they pay for basic things like food and their phones? Don't they all get bored being cooped up here all the time, tending to the veggie garden?

Shell looks a bit thrown by all the Funko Pops lined up against the walls and spread over basically every surface. 'Why does she keep everything in their boxes?'

Cath grins fondly. 'She sells and trades them online. Apparently they're worth more if you sell them unopened.'

Still so weird.

'I think it helps her feel like she's keeping them safe,' Cath murmurs, like the thought has just occurred to her.

There's a Pokémon blanket over the couch, and a matching doona cover on the bed. It's like how a thirteen-year-old would decorate a house if they could. Says a lot about her. A toolbox sits next to the couch, the same one I saw her with when Shell helped her fix the generator. Well, watched her fix it.

Shell runs her fingers over the windowsill, then shows me her clean finger. 'She's house proud.'

Greta seems strange, but I never thought that she'd be this . . . tidy. There's a real order here that I didn't expect. But how would she be if that order was threatened? I remember how she was yesterday with Walker. If he was a real threat to the life she had here, would she kill him to save it? Would any of them?

It's clear nobody is hiding in here. As Cath ushers us out the door, I look at Shell out of the corner of my eye. There's something up with her. I think she likes Greta, maybe even *like* likes her. It's hard to tell with Shell. She's my best friend, but she keeps her life to herself. I mean, it's not like I expect daily updates on being non-binary or having crushes, like her love life is a weather report, but still. It would be nice to know *something*.

I decide to leave it for now and focus on what we can learn from the residents by snooping through their cabins. These people have such distinct spaces. It's kind of funny, but it makes sense that each of their cabins is an external expression of them. I guess it just shows how different they are.

The next cabin is Maxine's. In contrast to the spareness of Tobias's cabin and the neatness of Greta's, Maxine's cabin looks like a zoo exploded inside it. There's animal print everywhere. Leopard, tiger, cougar, cheetah – all the major cats are represented here. The walls are covered in posters and tacky paintings of wildlife, some with pink feather boas hanging off the frames, and table lamps are draped with pink scarves. It's very . . . girly.

Shell looks horrified.

A quick look into her bedroom reveals more of the same. There's a big square mirror framed by light bulbs, like in a movie star's dressing room. Clothes are draped everywhere, on coat hangers, hooked on the doorknobs and curtain rails – all garish animal prints, hot pink, low cut, or all three.

Shell studies a plastic tree-shaped earring holder. 'That's a lot of ugly bling,' she mutters. 'But there's a pair of baguette diamond earrings that are nice, if they're real.' Shell's family has lots of money and her mother wears lots of jewellery, so I guess she'd know about this stuff, if only by osmosis.

Maxine seems quite chaotic as a person. I feel like she could be capable of anything given the right set of circumstances and amount of alcohol. I remember her flirting with Kane last night, but then how tired she seemed when he wasn't looking. Is all this animal print the real her, or just some elaborate costume? She is definitely not what she seems on the surface.

A few minutes later, Tobias and Cath come back out into the living room. He shakes his head. 'No one.'

As we wait for Cath to lock the cabin up behind us, I point to cabin four. 'What about that one?'

Tobias takes a key from Cath's hand. 'I'll just check myself. John won't mind me coming in, under the circumstance, but not you kids.'

How curious.

Tobias walks back to cabin four, and opens the door just wide enough to slip inside. In less than a minute he's back out, locking the door behind him and calling over to us. 'No one here either. Time to go back to the houseboat.'

Chapter 16

Jetty

The rain still isn't letting up, so we are half drenched by the time we reach the jetty, despite our umbrellas. In the light of day, it is eerie to see that it's the only houseboat around on a deserted expanse of lake. The water level seems much higher than yesterday, creeping up the sides of the jetty, steadily encroaching. How long before it rises up and floods the area between the lake and the cabins?

Cath rubs her neck. She looks a bit shaken, being back here, but she's doing her best to hide it.

The houseboat is a charred skeleton. The roof is buckled but hasn't caved in, and the windows are shattered in some places and warped into odd shapes elsewhere. There's a strange smell lingering in the air; a mix of chemicals, burnt wood and maybe charred upholstery.

Inside, most of the furniture has been reduced to indistinct lumps of ash and charred fabric, while other bits seem fine, just blackened. Electrical wires dangle from the ceiling, twisted and melted, their rubber casings dripping like wax. I can just make out a melted metal door handle, which looks fused to the wall.

Tobias tentatively climbs onto the houseboat again.

'What are you doing? It could be dangerous. And no one could be hiding here, we'd see them through the windows,' Cath says.

'I just want to check. You can't see the bedroom or bathroom from out here.'

He disappears for a moment, then reappears at the back of the houseboat where the engine is. He looks about, taking a couple of photos on his phone before making his way back to us.

He carefully steps over the railing and back onto the jetty, shaking his head. 'Nothing.'

I step a little too close to a burnt section of the jetty and almost lose my footing.

'Be careful!' yells Tobias, grabbing my arm to steady me.

I look down and see most of the planks nearest the houseboat are charred and crumbling, but I'm surprised there isn't more damage given what we saw last night. The metal fence along the jetty is blackened but still intact. The ropes that tied the houseboat to the fence are burnt but are somehow still holding, melted and glued to the rail post.

Glancing at the choppy water, I get flashbacks to nearly drowning last year. When I step sideways I realise I'm now standing where we found Walker's body. *Shit.* I feel myself start to shake. Tobias keeps his grip firm on my shoulder, and I try to focus on that instead.

'Do you think Walker started his engine to move his boat and somehow that triggered the gizmo you found?' asks Kane.

Tobias releases my shoulder and then rubs his chin. 'Maybe. It is also possible that he saw the fire and got caught when he tried to extinguish it.'

He tries his phone again, holding it up high and turning in circles. 'Still no signal. I would have thought it was clear enough to get satellite coverage now. I wonder if the booster got damaged in the storm?'

Shell looks over to the other side of the houseboat. 'If he got caught, why not just jump into the water? Why try to get out via the jetty?'

Cath is staring into the distance, with her arms wrapped around herself. 'He did tell me he wasn't a strong swimmer once.'

Shell plants her hands on her hips. 'What do you think Tobias? Was this fire deliberately lit?'

He pockets his phone with a sigh. 'Yes. And unless he set it himself and somehow got caught up in the fire, someone was clearly targeting Walker.'

Shell tilts her head to the side. 'Would he have done it himself for insurance money?'

'His family's rich, and the insurance would be maybe $50,000 at most,' Cath shakes her head when Kane lets out a whistle. 'That might seem like a lot to you and me, but trust me, it's nothing but spare change to the Walkers.'

'I don't know how to say this tactfully, but there's no way it could have been, um, suicide, is there?' Shell asks gently, directing her question at Cath.

Cath looks teary, but she speaks firmly. 'No. You saw him yesterday. He was full of ideas for the future. He was ambitious. He's the last person who would take his own life.'

Thinking about it, she's right. He seemed *so* alive yesterday, vibrant and cocky and dynamic. I know we didn't actually know him, but somehow I can't see him doing something like that.

Shell runs her hand across the blackened jetty rail. Her fingers come up black with charcoal. Tobias clears his throat. 'We should probably leave the jetty and the houseboat alone until the police are able to get through. Let's go back.'

As we turn to head back along the jetty, Tobias stops me with another gentle touch of my shoulder. I must be looking as shaky as I feel. 'Are you okay?'

'Yeah,' I say unconvincingly. 'It's just a lot. I came here looking for my mother. And instead, there's . . . all this, and I still don't know why someone told me to come here.'

He nods. 'Yes, I imagine this is quite a lot for you kids.'

'I'm not a kid. I've been through a lot. I just . . . I dunno.'

'Your family knows that you are here, don't they?' Tobias asks, concern in his voice.

'Yes, my adoptive mum knows. She's cool about it. She would have come too but she's got bad legs that are playing up right now. But I couldn't wait.'

'If she's okay with you doing this, she must be a good, understanding woman?'

I nod. 'Yeah, she is. It's been tricky lately, but we're good.' I don't want to go into the details with him. But it's true, things are good with Mum and me.

'Good to hear.'

Ahead of us, Cath turns and wipes the rain from her face. 'There's nothing more we can do here. I hate the thought that he tried to escape and his foot got caught—' she lets out a quiet sob. 'I'm sorry, it's just so awful.'

Tobias moves to her side and puts his arm around her. Cath rests her head on his shoulder, shaking with tears or the cold, or both. I walk over to Shell who is shivering too, and reach up to adjust her woolly cap so it's on more firmly. Kane seems oblivious to the cold.

'Caravan park next?' says Tobias.

Chapter 17

Caravans

We walk back along the track we drove up yesterday and then head right toward the caravan park. It takes about fifteen minutes because we're all walking fairly gingerly, trying not to slip in the mud. The sign out the front reads 'Walker's Lake Getaway Park'.

There's row upon row of unoccupied parking spaces, fifty at least. It's eerily empty and feels sinister, like a post-apocalyptic version of a caravan park. If a group of zombies came lumbering out from behind one of the trailers, it wouldn't look out of place. There are a few permanent caravans around, as well as a collection of cabins at the back of the block. There's a small office at the front with a sign on the door saying 'Closed due to storm' in shaky writing, like it was scrawled in a hurry, and there are a couple of old red-brick toilet and shower blocks. But otherwise it's deserted. There are no cars here, which suggests that everyone must have left ahead of the storm, like Vince said.

Shell is looking around in fascination. Her family is rich, and her parents only like the best of the best, so it's a pretty safe bet to assume she would never have stayed anywhere as basic as a caravan park before. She seems very down to earth, but every now and then her wealth peeks through.

Tobias and Cath walk up and down the empty aisles between the lots, marked out by white lines and crumpled grass. They knock on the doors of the few caravans that are still here, stickybeaking through the windows where they can. No response.

'They all seem locked,' I hear Cath say. 'I don't see how anyone could hide here without breaking in, and there's no sign of that.'

Tobias nods in agreement. 'Unless they already had a key, but that seems unlikely. If you were going to commit this crime, staying here would be a bit of a giveaway.'

Shell, Kane and I head to the park office. When we get to the door it's clear that it's all locked up. Like Vince's shop, the office seems to belong to a different time. Red bricks, a broken awning hanging crookedly above the door, old fashioned bell attached to the door. Signs in the window that have faded with time, advertising lake activities with photos from years ago. There's no one here.

As Cath and Tobias join us at the office, Kane points toward the road leading back down to the boom gate. 'I might go down and see if Walker's car is still stuck there, and see if anyone can get through yet.'

'Good idea,' I say. He smiles and plods off through the park. 'Don't get caught up in the water!' I yell after him. He salutes and stomps on through the rain, disappearing from view.

'If everyone left because the storm was coming, why did you all stay?' I ask Cath.

She puts her hands in her jean pockets. 'We're further up the hill than the others and we thought we'd escape the worst of any flooding. Plus, unlike most people here, this is our home and we wanted to stay and protect it. But given how things have turned out, I wish we had left. Maybe I'm too stubborn for my own good.'

'Vince at the shop said you were all crazy to stay,' I say.

She chuckles wryly. 'Vince would say that.'

As we near the bottom of the hill, Kane comes into view, trudging back up the road, his pants drenched all the way up above the knee. He must have waded through the water blocking the entry.

'His Merc is there, bogged in near the gate. The entry's still completely flooded. There's still no way a car could get in or out of here.'

Shell and I look at each other.

'We're cut off from everyone,' Kane says.

I glance around this deserted place and suddenly feel quite scared.

'And nobody is hiding here, or at The Circle,' Tobias says, his voice tinged with resignation, or maybe something else. 'Which means that one of us did this.'

Chapter 18

Cushion

Ten minutes later we're all sitting in Cath's lounge room again, like we're stuck in some kind of endless TV rerun. We've all dried off, and Kane is now wearing a pair of Nash's pants.

'You're giving away all of my clothes,' Nash mutters, turning back to his Nintendo. I notice that his tongue is hanging out a little in concentration as he plays, like a little kid. It's oddly cute.

Cath is standing in the kitchen again, both arms rigid and straining against the kitchen bench. There's a pile of streamers by her arm that someone has started to take down.

Maxine's hair is as limp as her wrinkled leopard print shirt. She's drinking from a water bottle, and it crosses my mind that it might be vodka. I used to suspect Mum of the same thing.

Greta's eyes are dark and bagged, magnified by her big glasses. She looks skittish, as if worried someone might jump out at any moment and attack her.

Tobias is of course reading a book. But every now and then he makes eye contact with Cath and her concerned expression matches his.

My anxiety feels like it's through the roof: my heart is racing, and I feel fishhooks in my stomach, pulling and tangling inside of me. Everyone must be thinking the same thing but no one is saying it. I can't bear it anymore. I'm holding a green couch cushion in front of me, both to hide my stomach and to squeeze like a stress toy.

'It must be one of us!' I blurt out, unable to stop myself.

It sure has an impact. It's as if time has frozen, like even the dust particles trapped in the light have stopped moving. Everyone is looking at me in shock, even Tobias, even though he said the same thing when we were at the caravan park.

Greta is the first to react, making this little yelping sound. 'No, no way!' her eyes are wilder than ever as she starts shaking like a terrified dog at an animal shelter.

Maxine reaches out to her. 'You've upset her now,' she hisses at me.

Cath comes into the lounge area to sit on the other side of Greta. 'Gus, was that really necessary?'

Nash is grinning at me. I can't figure out if he thinks it's cool I said it or if he's laughing because I upset Greta.

Shell's leg won't stop jiggling against her chair. 'We looked everywhere, including the caravan park. From what we can tell, there's no one else here. It's the only logical conclusion.'

'They have to be hiding somewhere else then,' says Maxine, a little too loudly. My vodka theory feels a bit more likely now.

'There's still no way in or out, and we've checked everywhere,' Kane says. 'All of the cabins are empty.'

'Did you check the stone circle?' asks Greta.

Tobias closes his book with a snap. 'We did not check there, but how could they stay out all night in the rain, and hide behind the stones during the day?'

Greta is agitated, shaking her head as Maxine and Cath try to soothe her. 'Well, maybe they were in the other cabin and then hid in the stones in the morning before anyone saw them?'

'We looked in that cabin too, but there was no sign anyone had been there. Not even a footprint.' Tobias points to the wet footprints all over the entrance to Cath's cabin.

It's not impossible, but it seems unlikely. Then again, the whole thing seems unlikely. My head aches. I want to just go back to bed and sleep until the rain stops and the floodwaters recede and we can get out of here.

I'm about to suggest we go when suddenly Shell pulls her phone out and holds it up. 'I've worked out a rough timeline. Maybe we could go through it and see if there's a way to eliminate anyone.'

Cath scoffs. 'Who do you think you are?'

Shell ignores her question. 'I'll start. I got here at about 5.30 and helped Greta set up the food. I was here when everyone else arrived. It was 6.45 when I went out for a smoke and saw the fire. We don't know when it started, but it may have been around 6.25 when Tobias heard that booming sound on his way here. It makes sense then that we should see where everyone was around that time, right Tobias?'

'Yes, I suppose,' Tobias replies.

'Okay, great.' Shell turns away from him and focuses on the three women sitting on the couch. 'Let's start with you, Cath.'

Cath jumps to her feet and jabs her finger at Shell. She looks furious. 'It's not up to you to question any of us.'

'We didn't know Walker, so we're the only people here who don't have a motive,' Shell responds calmly, implying they all do have a motive, of course.

Tobias steps in, his palms raised in an effort to get them to calm down. 'If you kids are determined to play detective, at least let us all go back to our cabins for a bit to change clothes and have some peace and quiet. You can talk to each of us in turn. I'm sure Cath in particular wants some peace in this cabin. Does everyone agree?'

Again, that look passes between Tobias and Cath. What do they know that they aren't saying?

On the couch, Maxine and Greta nod in agreement. Nash just scowls, as usual.

Cath turns to Greta, hands on hips. 'Do you think you could go and look at the satellite booster, Greta? It might help us get the signal back. The sooner we can call the *real* police, the better.'

Greta bobs her head up and down furiously, probably pleased to have something to do. She scuttles out of the cabin with Tobias following. Nash disappears back into his room. Maxine stands and walks a little unsteadily to the door, leaving the three of us with Cath.

'Right, so you're going to interrogate me, are you?' she says coldly, finding a chair on the opposite side of the room. She's set herself up as far away from us as possible.

'Not interrogate, just ask a few questions.' Shell holds her own. She's so impressive. I can feel myself cowering under Cath's glare.

'As I said, I got here at 5.30 to set up the party with Greta, but you weren't here.'

Cath crosses her arms across her chest. 'I was probably getting some carrots and celery from the garden to chop up for the dips.'

'Did anyone see you?' Shell asks.

'I don't know. The garden is closest to this cabin, and on the far side of the property, so it's possible no one saw me.'

Shell nods, tapping notes into her phone. 'Can you tell me who came to the party and in what order?'

Cath frowns, clearly annoyed. Maybe it's the questions, maybe because it's Shell asking them. Either way, I feel like she's used to telling people what to do, rather than having her own movements questioned.

'When I came back here you and Greta were setting up the snacks. Nash was in his room, avoiding work of course. We said the party would start at 6 pm, and everyone arrived close to then.'

'Who got here first?' Shell pushes.

'Hmm. Maxine arrived maybe five minutes early with extra drinks. Then Gus and Kane. Tobias turned up next, with a book, which I found frustratingly typical. I think he got here around 6.30. But I can't be sure of any of this, since we're not really clock watchers here.'

'Of course,' I say. 'Thanks. Is there anything else you can think of?'

Cath shakes her head. 'No. Once we were all here, no one left.'

'Except Nash, who at some point saw the fire, and then left the cabin to look at it?' Shell says pointedly.

Cath scowls at her. 'Well, yes.'

Kane, who has been unusually quiet, suddenly pipes up. 'It only took us ten minutes to walk to the jetty in the storm. I reckon someone could sneak out, set fire to the houseboat, and be back here without anyone noticing. They wouldn't need to be gone long.'

'I think we'd notice,' Cath says dryly. 'When Shell went out the entire room became Arctic.'

'We didn't notice Nash leave,' I say quietly.

There is a short silence. *Now's as good a time as ever.*

I take out my phone and hold up the photo of Jane again. 'I feel like you didn't get a good look at this picture of Jane when we got here yesterday. This is an old picture, but are you sure you don't know her?'

Cath looks at the photo closely and shakes her head.

Shell changes tack. 'Might Jane have a connection to John in cabin four?'

'Why would you think that?' Cath asks, her eyes fiery.

'We're just trying to understand why someone would tell Gus to come here to find Jane.'

Cath shrugs, her mouth set in a thin line. She's run out of patience now.

'Last thing. Who do *you* think did this?' Shell asks.

Cath looks surprised, her mouth dropping open a little before she composes herself.

'I don't believe anyone in The Circle could have done it. The most likely person is, honestly, one of you. But as you said, you only just met Simon yesterday, so I don't see why you would do it either.'

Shell goes to respond, but I get in first, standing up and smiling. 'Thanks Cath. I know this is all so strange, us turning up out of the blue and asking about Jane, and now this. Thanks for putting us up and for answering our questions.'

Cath stands too, patting her hands down her jeans. 'It's not a game you know. Someone has died.'

We all nod, our eyes on the floor. Just as we're all about to go out the door, Shell turns back to Cath. 'What was your relationship like with Simon?'

Cath freezes, sucking her teeth. 'I beg your pardon?'

Shell tilts her head to the side. 'Everyone else was furious at him yesterday, but you were much more reasonable. Why?'

Cath stares at her. Shell stares back.

The silence is only broken by Nash emerging from his bedroom, where he has clearly been listening. He makes his way to the middle of the room, anger on his face.

'Because they were hooking up!' he snarls.

Chapter 19

Nintendo

'Nash!' snaps Cath in horror.

'Like it isn't true. I know what you were up to.'

Cath looks both furious and embarrassed. The colour rises in her cheeks and her fists are clenched by her side. If looks could kill, Nash would be dead on the floor. But he just stands there, Nintendo in hand, completely unfazed.

'Admit it. You were together. You'd go into town for "supplies" but you were really going in to meet him.'

Cath collapses on the couch, like the wind has been knocked out of her.

'Oh God. Yes, it's true. And now he's dead!' she moans, tears forming in her eyes. Nash looks a bit guilty now, his own face going red. Then he looks at his feet, like a badly behaved child, which is basically what he is. I suddenly feel sorry for him.

Cath wipes her eyes and then starts picking at the thread on her jumper again. 'I knew it was just his way of trying to get me to sell. I was under no illusions.'

Nash rolls his eyes and turns away. She stares at him, desperately trying to get him to look at her.

'We understood each other.'

Shell looks sceptical, eyebrow raised. 'Did he sway you? It sounded like you were adamant you weren't going to sell yesterday.'

'No!'

There's a loaded silence. Shell seems poised to ask another question but holds back. I want to ask more too, but am not sure whether to push it or not. I've learned that if you wait in a silence long enough, someone starts talking.

As if on cue, Cath continues. 'I just enjoyed his company,' she says softly. 'I love it here, don't get me wrong, but it was nice to go out for dinner every now and then, get some attention. Sometimes we'd go out on the lake in his houseboat for the afternoon. It was always so peaceful.'

She is such a strong, grounded figure that I find it hard to picture her dating Walker, someone so shiny and domineering. Maybe there's more to her than I realise.

'He was playing you,' Nash mutters.

She nods at him. 'I knew he was just doing it to get the land. I'm not a fool. I just didn't care. And I genuinely think he enjoyed our time together, despite his agenda.'

'Tobias said something about his father yesterday,' I say.

'Yes, Bartholomew Walker is a piece of work, much more full-on than Simon is . . . was. He's a big deal around these parts. Owns half of Walliss, and Marrell, the nearby township, as well. Simon was very much in his shadow.'

She keeps fiddling with the loose thread of her jumper. 'I remember one night we were out to dinner when Bartholomew came rolling in with a group of other businessmen, all quite pissed. They were loud and obnoxious. When they saw us together, they gave him a hard time about playing soft, not being ruthless enough. Simon's confidence fell away in front of me. Then, almost to rub salt into the wound, Bartholomew patted him on the head and told him he was only joking.'

He sounds like a creep.

Nash opens his mouth, then swiftly closes it again. I wonder what's on his mind. I wonder a lot of things about him.

'How did you get this joint in the first place?' Kane asks.

'Yes,' says Shell, 'especially since the stone circle might be historically significant. Did you consult with First Nations people or compensate them?'

'That's enough. I'm only tolerating these questions because a crime has been committed,' Cath snaps at Shell.

The thread she's been fiddling with breaks off in her fingers. She looks at it, annoyed, and then at Shell as if it was her fault it broke.

'We're not trying to be invasive, but I can't help feeling that this property and the crime are connected,' I say, trying to take the heat out of the situation.

Cath sighs. 'Alright then. I bought the land without even knowing the stone circle was here. There was no mention of it in any of the paperwork. I wanted to get away from the city,' she looks at Nash sidelong. He avoids her gaze. 'I worked in real estate, so I just put some feelers out and this property came up. An elderly lady had owned it for over forty years, with the cabins all in disrepair. She was keen to sell to me because she didn't want Simon's father to get it. He would have destroyed the bushland to expand the caravan park. That's why Simon was so keen to get it, to impress his father.'

'And did his father want the circle too?' I ask.

'No one knew about the circle then. There was incredible overgrowth everywhere, especially further up the hill. The previous owner might have forgotten it existed, or maybe she never knew it was there.'

'What was it like, discovering it?' I ask.

Cath's face changes in an instant as she smiles broadly at me, her eyes shining. 'It was amazing! I had been here for months by that stage, slowly repairing the cabins. It was clear that summer was coming and that I need to start building a bushfire plan. I paid a landscaper from town to come in with a digger and do the heavy work around the perimeter of the property, clearing the worst of the overgrowth. Then on the second day, he hit something and the digger's blade got stuck. And there it was, this unusual stone. We hacked back the foliage and uncovered another, then another.'

'Wow, that's so cool,' I say. 'It must have been so exciting, like an archaeological dig. That sense of real discovery, of uncovering something ancient that had been forgotten.'

She laughs. 'It was certainly a big moment for me. Well, us, even though Nash won't admit it.'

'Whatever,' he says, but there's a smile underneath his dismissal.

'It's why we named our community The Circle, out of respect for the stones,' she smiles at Nash before continuing with the story. 'I contacted people in town to try and see if there was a local Indigenous group who knew anything about it. There weren't any. But I did some googling and found Tobias, so I contacted him.'

It's all starting to come together now. I wonder how the others came to be here, but figure I can ask them when we talk to them next.

Suddenly she stands up. 'Right, that's it. Enough with the questions. I'm done,' she says forcefully, grabbing her phone off the kitchen counter. 'I'm going to go up the hill and see if I can get a signal. I'll leave you kids to "interview" Nash.' She pulls on a jacket, slamming the door on her way out.

Nash flops down on the couch in the space Cath has left. He snorts as his mother leaves. 'You lot are so cringe, you know that, right? Why should I talk to you?' He folds his arms across his chest and spreads his legs a bit, looking like one of Kane's gym poses that he can't stop posting on socials.

'Well, for starters, we literally solved an actual crime last year, so we know what we're doing. Plus, we're the only ones without a motive,' I say, trying to sound tougher than I feel.

His ears prick up at the mention of a crime but he doesn't say anything. He just glares at me. I glare back. It's a game of chicken. Suddenly something passes across his eyes and he looks away.

'Okay then, what's my motive?' he challenges me. 'I want to get out of this shithole, so why would I hurt the one person who could make that happen?'

Good point. 'So what's stopping you?'

He goes quiet. 'I can't, not just yet. Mum needs me.' He runs his hand through his hair.

'Why does she need you?'

'That's private.'

I'm getting nowhere with this, so I try to think back to yesterday. 'Why'd you throw that sand at Walker?'

'Why do you think? He thinks he's hot shit and he's not.'

'Thought,' Shell says automatically.

He looks at her, surprised. 'What?'

'He *thought* he was hot shit. He's gone, remember?'

Nash looks out the window. 'Yeah, I know.' There seems to be a tinge of something in his voice. Sadness? Regret?

'So, if wanting to stay here isn't a motive, then maybe you hated him because he was messing around with your mum?'

Nash glares at me again. 'Why would I care about that? I don't care what she does, or who she does,' he spits, but there's too much fire behind it. I don't believe him.

'Okay. What time did you leave the party last night? I don't remember seeing you here till later on.'

He smirks at me. 'Watching me, were you? Like what you see?'

I can feel myself blushing a little. He's figuring me out faster than I can figure myself out. I find myself wishing for Kane or Shell to pipe up with questions of their own, to take the heat off of me.

His smirk deepens as my face reddens. 'I snuck out my window after everyone had arrived, maybe around 6.40.'

'Why'd you leave the cabin in the middle of a storm?'

'I needed to get something from the garage, and then I saw the fire so I went to have a look.' His eyes are shifty now, like he's nervous about something.

Shell tries a different approach. 'Walker seemed to have it all. Looks, hot car, money. You were jealous of him, weren't you? Having all of that and your mother's attention as well.'

'No I wasn't!'

Shell knows when she's found a weak spot. 'You expect us to believe that you just happened to sneak out on the same night someone set fire to his houseboat? Is that really a coincidence?'

This hits home. His smirk has morphed into anger. 'It's the truth! I saw the fire and went to see what was happening.'

'Without telling anyone? Did you light it?' I ask. He's acting really strange.

'You lot need to leave, now!' he shouts, marching back into his room and slamming the door.

The three of us look at one another.

'That was weird,' says Kane.

'Why would he do that? Just stand there watching, not raising the alarm at all, if he wasn't responsible? It doesn't make sense,' I whisper.

Kane snickers. 'Because he's a nut job.'

'Keep it down, these walls are pretty thin,' Shell says, drumming her fingers on her thigh. 'He was staring at the fire like he was hypnotised. But does that automatically mean he lit it?'

'Yes,' says Kane.

'I dunno,' I say. 'I thought he looked paralysed, like he'd gone there and seen Walker's body and just froze.'

Shell nods. 'We can't just assume he did it. But his reaction was full-on.'

'He seems to get angry easily,' I say. 'Who should we speak to next?'

'Maxine,' says Kane. 'Greta,' says Shell.

'Tobias it is then,' I laugh.

Chapter 20

Professor

The rain is easing now, but the wind is still bitterly cold. I stand under the verandah of Cath's cabin and stare out across the expanse. I can't believe last night it was raining so heavily that we could barely see a metre in front of us. If Shell hadn't gone outside, we may not have seen the houseboat at all until today. Although I guess Nash would have said something, eventually.

While the thought of Walker being burnt hits me hard, the thought of his burnt body being left alone in the storm all night is somehow even worse. I shiver.

On the walk to Tobias's house, my hands are sweating, despite the cold. 'Is it just me, or do you guys find it creepy that there's a dead body in his cabin?'

'A hundred per cent,' says Kane.

I wipe the moisture from my face. 'I'm worried it will smell.'

Shell raises her hand to knock when suddenly the front door opens. Tobias moves to let us in. 'Come in will you, and stop talking nonsense on the doorstep.'

We go back into his cabin, feeling chastised.

'I suppose it is my turn to play suspect to your detectives?' he asks in a patronising way, hands on his hips.

'Yes, actually,' I say. 'We're trying to confirm our timeline. So, let's start with where were you around 6 pm?'

'Washing my glass eye,' he says, scratching his head.

There's an awkward silence. Tobias must see the confused look on my face. 'I am joking, obviously.'

He certainly seems cheerier than yesterday, which is odd given the circumstances. He's hard to figure out.

'I was here, revising my book and trying to think of a reason not to go to the party. But it seemed rude not to go, given it was Cath's birthday. And I was curious about you kids.'

'Curious how?' asks Shell.

'Your story about looking for your mother, Gus. I wanted to know more.'

'We can get to that,' I say. 'So, you're saying that at 6 pm you were here, alone?'

'Yes.'

'And when did you arrive at the party?'

'I'm not sure. Maybe 6.30? I'm a bit vague on the actual times.'

'You have no real alibi then?'

'Well, I didn't know I needed one, did I?' he says wryly.

True.

'Tell us about how you came to be living here,' says Shell.

'Cath contacted me when she found the stone circle. I am quite easy to find if you google me.'

'And you came right here and moved in?'

'Hardly. I did come relatively quickly to see what she had found and to make sure, if it was real, that she didn't damage the circle in any way. These rare circles must be protected. And this one just appearing one day, without any records about it, was an amazing find.'

'How can no one know about it?' asks Shell.

'Well, there are very few First Nations folk living around here now, and the only ones I've been able to contact know nothing about this circle, other than the academic I told you about. Elders must have moved on, by force or by choice, or passed away years ago, and with them went the knowledge about the circle. It sounds like the owner before Cath may not have known it existed either.'

He sighs before continuing. 'This was all before the 1993 *Native Title Act*, so First Nations' land ownership was far more nebulous back then. It was a different time. Though, in some ways, not that much different to now, sadly.'

'Once you saw the circle was legit, what did you do?' asks Kane.

'I arranged some research leave from my university and came here to do a proper survey. And I contacted a First Nations researcher I knew vaguely in a different region. She is actually coming up here soon to work with me.'

'That's good,' says Shell.

Now that we've got him taking the conversation seriously, it seems like a good time to get into the real questions.

'Yesterday it seemed like you were pretty angry with Walker,' I say.

Tobias frowns. 'Well, you heard what he said about buying this land and turning the circle into some kind of tourist gimmick. The man was an ignorant capitalist, but it does not mean I wanted to kill him.'

He looks to the door of his spare bedroom. We all follow his gaze. It's so odd being here, having this conversation about Walker, when his body is literally in the next room.

I start to feel shaky again. My stomach is churning, and I feel like the breath is leaving my body. I feel a panic attack coming on. The thought of him in there while we're talking about him, calling him an idiot, is making me feel sick.

There's something filling my nostrils that I can't name. 'Is that . . . can you guys smell him?'

Kane and Shell shake their heads.

Can he hear us? I know it makes no sense but what if he can? He's so close.

Shell touches my hand. 'You okay?'

'How much is the stone circle worth?' Kane asks, trying to distract from how strange I'm acting. Tobias looks at him like he's mad.

'Worth? It's of massive cultural significance. It's *priceless*.'

'Yeah, but how much was Walker prepared to pay for it?' Kane persists.

Tobias frowns. 'He wanted the land so he could redevelop it into holiday accommodation, extend his father's caravan park right up here. He was not really interested in the stones, per se, just their value as an attraction.'

I find that so surprising I forget I was having a panic attack. Couldn't he see that it was magic or mystical or . . . something? Every time I think about the stones, I feel the circle almost pull me toward it.

Tobias is staring at me intently. I can't figure out if he's angry or confused or something else. 'Do you feel something when you look at the stones?'

Is he a mind reader? 'Yes, there's something about them. Do you guys feel it too?' I turn to Shell and Kane.

'They're intriguing, sure, but not really,' Shell replies, shrugging.

'Nothing,' says Kane.

'Oh. Well, there is something, but I can't explain it.'

'Indeed. For now, my focus is trying to get an historical cultural overlay put in place to stop any development of this land. It won't stop a land sale, but it means that anyone who does buy this land will not be able to touch the stones. It is more about keeping the site safe until I can at least consult with Indigenous people of this land and see what they want to do. It is their culture, their history . . . sorry, I sound like I am giving a lecture, but it is important that it is *their* decision.'

Kane looks puzzled. 'Does that mean Cath has bought the land illegally?'

'No, she has a legitimate claim. But it is more complex than that and depends on what local and state government rules are in place.'

I've been staring at the painting of the circle while they've been talking. Tobias sees me looking. 'When I looked at it yesterday, I swore it changed colour,' I say without thinking.

Tobias goes to say something, stops, then starts again. 'John is a clever painter.'

'What brought him to this community?'

'You can ask him yourself. I am sure he will return as soon as the floodwaters recede.'

Why do Tobias and Cath keep avoiding this question?

'It's quite sinister,' says Shell, peering at the painting more closely.

Tobias laughs. 'Much like the circle itself, in a certain light.'

Even now, the colours of the landscape seem to shift and change. 'Can you guys see that? It's like a live photo, but in paint!'

'I can't see anything,' Kane says.

'How can you not see it, it's so clear?'

'I just can't, okay!' snaps Kane angrily.

Why is he suddenly so crabby? Maybe this whole situation is starting to affect him too. It would make sense, but it's so unlike him.

Tobias just watches us like he's observing lab rats navigate a maze.

Chapter 21

Lizard

The rain has stopped now and there's almost a hint of sun as we step outside. The wind has less of a bite to it, so it's starting to feel less freezing as we move on toward Greta's cabin. It's behind Cath's, and it seems smaller somehow. I'm still thinking about Kane's outburst from before.

'You get on well with her,' I say to Shell, 'Did you want to take the lead? She likes you, but I think Kane or me will just spook her.'

Shell nods. Kane hangs back with me as she knocks on the door. At first there's no answer. Then I see that she's opening the front window curtain a little to see who it is. I touch Shell's arm and point toward the window.

'Greta, we just wanted to see if you're okay. And check some stuff with you,' Shell calls out.

She opens the door like an old woman afraid of being robbed, eyes wide as always behind her enormous glasses.

'Is it okay if we come in?' Shell asks gently.

I remember when I was young, I was sitting in the garden once with Mum when she suddenly nudged me. 'Don't move,' she whispered. 'There's a lovely lizard watching us by the gate.' I really slowly moved just my eyes, not my head, looking over at the gate. Right by the fencepost there was a lizard staring at us. So cool, like a baby dinosaur or something.

The lizard watched us so intently, eyes doing that slow reptilian blinking thing before they make their sudden movements.

Greta pokes her head out the door. 'Okay, come in,' she says, darting in again. With her big unblinking eyes and her erratic movements, she reminds me of that lizard.

Inside, it feels like her Funko Pops are watching me.

I notice her toolbox on the floor, at the foot of the coffee table. It's open and I can see a box cutter knife sitting on the top next to a hammer. There's something sitting next to the toolbox, a lump hidden under a hand towel. I can't tell what it is without making it obvious I'm snooping.

'Sit,' she says. 'What do you wanna know?'

We all have a seat on her couch.

Shell settles in her spot and smiles at her. 'We just wanted to go through the times from last night. Cath said it was okay, remember?'

She nods warily, blinking extra slowly. Such lizard vibes.

'Okay, great. We were at Cath's together, right?'

'Yes. You helped me with the food and decorations.'

Shell nods. 'I got there around 5.30, and you were the only person there. Do you remember who came in after me?'

'Maxine was first. Then the boys,' she points at Kane and me. 'Then Tobias.'

'What about Cath?'

'She was in the garden.'

'And Nash?'

'Dunno. Why don't you ask him?'

'We will.'

She frowns and begins picking at her nails. 'He'll just lie anyway, I reckon.'

'What does he lie about?'

'*Everything.*'

'Like?'

'Ask him why they moved here.' She seems quite angry all of a sudden, her hands forming little fists in her lap.

'Okay, I will,' says Shell. I can see her mind ticking over. She nods to my pocket, and I get the hint. I pull out my phone and turn the screen to Greta.

'This is a picture of my mother, Jane. Do you recognise her?'

Greta stands up suddenly. 'You should go now. I've got things to do.'

Shell smiles at her again. 'Okay, we'll go. But just one more thing. Why did you dislike Walker so much?'

Greta kicks the leg of the coffee table. 'He wanted to wreck this place, to kick us out. Where would I go? This is all I have.' I can see tears forming in her eyes, magnified by her glasses. The wetness makes her look even more like a lizard.

'Cath said she'd never sell,' Kane says. She looks at him in surprise, like she just realised he was here.

'Things change, whether you want them to or not.'

'How did you meet Cath and come to live here?' Shell asks gently.

Greta smiles and seems to settle, lowering herself back down onto her seat. 'When I left school, I used to clean her real estate office. Sometimes I'd fix things for her. I was living in a care home but I hated it, so I was looking for a new place to live. She invited me to come and help her fix up these cabins to rent out.'

While Shell is getting her to talk, I pretend to 'accidentally' bump Greta's toolbox with my leg, making the hammer, a roll of duct tape and the box cutter spill out onto the carpet.

'Careful!' she says, annoyed.

'Sorry,' I say, putting the tools back into the toolbox, but quickly sliding the box cutter into my sock and covering it with the hem of my jeans. A flash of white catches my eye, and I notice that the towel has slipped a little, revealing part of a clock mechanism. I remember Tobias saying she wasn't as good at fixing stuff as she claimed.

Poor Greta. She must be hiding the clock, embarrassed because she can't fix it. I suddenly feel sorry for her. Shell has Greta's full attention, and I'm glad she hasn't noticed what I've seen. I nudge the towel back over the clock bits.

Shell is speaking quietly, trying to keep Greta calm. 'What would make Cath change her mind about selling The Circle?'

'Nash might.' She narrows her eyes behind her glasses and points to the door.

'We're leaving now, but one last thing. Who do you think did this?' asks Shell, almost whispering, trying one more time as she moves to stand.

'I don't know.'

'Was anyone acting suspicious last night?' Shell persists. This time she seems to get a small reaction. Shell pauses at the edge of her seat. 'What do you want to tell me?'

Greta bites her bottom lip. 'I saw Maxine burying something in the garden last night.'

'What was it?'

'I could only see her back and the pitchfork, not what she was burying.'

'Thanks Greta,' Shell says with a big smile, gesturing for Kane and me to follow her out the door. We've overstayed our welcome.

'Wow. She's *so* weird,' Kane says once we're outside.

Shell shakes her head. 'She's just a bit different, that's all.'

'Fancy her do you?' he laughs.

Shell gives him a death stare that could bring down a government. 'No. I just have empathy. You should try it.'

'Stop it, you two. We need to follow up about that pitchfork and nighttime digging. We still have one more interview.'

Chapter 22

Leopard

Maxine opens the door to her cabin with a glass of wine in her hand. It's only 11 am.

'We just had a murder on our doorstep, so I'm allowed a drink,' she sneers at me after following my gaze.

She turns to Kane. 'Join me, handsome?'

Even he looks a little taken aback, but he laughs it off.

'I'm good thanks. But I do want to ask you some questions.'

'Yeah, yeah, sure.' She waves us through the door.

Maxine drapes herself on her couch like she's posing for a photographer. I guess it's meant to be seductive, but she just looks uncomfortable. Kane smiles at her though, which seems to be all she wants.

'You sure I can't tempt you?' she asks Kane. 'With a drink I mean, luv,' she winks.

He shakes his head, clearly uncomfortable. 'No thanks. I'd like to know what time you got to the party yesterday?'

'I don't know for sure, but I'd say it was just before 6 pm. I had to bring over some extra drinks because we'd invited these strange kids who rocked up out of nowhere!'

Kane manages a smile. 'Sorry about that. What about before the party?'

'I was here getting ready. It takes time to look this good,' she giggles.

Shell inhales sharply next to me, as if she's going to get snarky. I touch her arm gently. We need this, and Kane is doing well with Maxine. Shell exhales slowly, her eyes closed.

Kane presses on. 'Who was there when you arrived?'

'Greta and Shell were,' she says, tapping a talon on her wineglass. 'I think Cath was in the kitchen, but I'm not sure.'

'Where was Nash?'

'I assumed he was in his room.'

Kane nods, then follows Shell's lead. This is the first time he's asked the questions, and I'm impressed at how good he is at it. 'What did you think of Walker?'

Her eyes narrow and she takes a swig of wine. 'He was a bastard. Arrogant.'

'He was quite handsome,' I say. I feel like there's something more behind her comments.

'Oh yes, he was good-looking, but he knew it. He thought he was too good for the likes of us.' She fiddles with her dangly earrings.

'Did you fancy him?' I ask, in a *just between us* kind of way.

'Don't be ridiculous,' she snaps, over the top. Calming herself, she adds, 'Not my type at all.'

Kane smiles softly at her. 'He made some pretty harsh comments the other day. That must have hurt.'

Suddenly the flirty performance falls away, just like at the party, and she takes another gulp of wine. 'Yes, it did. I've made some bad decisions in my life, hurt people I love. But I've paid for those mistakes. How dare he use my family as a weapon against me?'

'Are you comfortable telling us what happened to your family?' Shell asks.

Maxine looks at her, then gets up and walks to the fridge, returning with an overfull glass.

'That's a two-glass story, luv,' she says, raising her drink in a mock toast. She sits back down again, more naturally this time, curled up but not posing.

'I got married young. Right out of high school. Bought a house, had a kid, did the things you're meant to do. And it was fine. Really, it was. Until it wasn't. I had this itch . . . this nagging feeling that I couldn't shake.' She tightens her grip on the wineglass, and I notice she hasn't replaced the nail that fell off the other day. 'I just kept looking at my tidy house and my tidy life, thinking *is this it?* It wasn't enough.'

None of us speak. It's hard to know what to say, but Maxine saves us, filling the silence.

'My daughter caught me one day crying in the kitchen. She asked why I was sad, and without thinking I just told her I wanted *more.* I'd never said it out loud before, but there it was.'

She sighs. 'So, I started having a drink in the arvo before I had to pick my daughter up from school. Then another and another and another.' She holds her glass up high in a mock-toast. 'I became the drunk housewife cliche, smiling for her family but drinking herself stupid in secret.

'In the end, my husband left and took my daughter with him. I was on my own, just me and the booze. I was in a bad way. That's when I happened to meet Cath and Greta in town one day, and Cath took me under her wing . . .' her voice drifts off as she stares sadly into her glass.

She's lost her family, just like I have.

Kane has done really well to get her to open up like this. Seems like Walker knew her secrets. *How did he find out?*

'I'm sorry to hear that, Maxine,' says Shell.

'It's okay. I've been burying this for a long time,' she smiles, wiping a tear from her cheek.

Burying. Shell cracks her fingers. 'Funny you should say that. Someone said they saw you burying something last night in the garden.'

Maxine baulks awkwardly. 'No. Why would I be messing about in the garden in the middle of a storm?'

I've got nothing. Shell drops it.

We sit in silence for a while. This is my cue. I pull up the photo of Jane.

'This is my mother.'

Maxine takes the phone from my hand and looks closely at it. 'She's pretty.'

I nod. 'I've been looking for her. Have you seen her?'

She avoids my eyes and turns to look out the window toward the lake. 'The rain has finally stopped. It's that lovely moment between rain and sun. I could live in this moment for years,' she says softly.

We silently follow her gaze, seeing the sun poking through the grey sky.

I'm about to ask her the question again, when suddenly all of our phones start to ping. Missed call notifications and text messages start filling up my screen.

'It's over,' says Maxine, standing up and moving to the window, scrolling through her phone. Does she mean the storm, or her moment between rain and sun? Or something else entirely?

Chapter 23

Cupboard

Back in our cabin, we all get on our phones. I call Mum who must have been trying to get through every minute since I left, based on the number of missed calls.

'Gussy,' she yelps. 'Are you alright? I heard the news about the storm up there and when I couldn't get hold of you, I started to panic. Fiona and Cheryl are worried sick about Kane and Shell. I wish you'd waited the extra week to go up there.'

She clearly has been worried, and she doesn't even know about the body yet. Tobias will be telling the police now, and they'll take over, but I should tell her now before she eventually hears about it on the news. I made a commitment not to lie to her after last year, when I made Kane and Shell come with me to solve the cold case behind her back.

'Everyone's on their phones to their parents right now,' I take a deep breath. 'I have to tell you something important, Mum. We're all okay, but there was an . . . accident here last night.'

She's silent for two seconds. 'What kind of accident?'

There's no point delaying it, so I jump right in. 'A houseboat caught fire and a man was killed.'

I feel like I'm underplaying it, but I don't want to make it into an even bigger deal for her and have her panic when she can't get here. Tobias and Cath will be reporting what happened to the police as we speak. Once they arrive it will all be fine.

'Oh my God,' she shrieks. I almost have to take the phone away from my ear it's so loud. 'What happened? Are you all okay? Tell me everything.'

I take her through the events of the last twenty-four hours. She makes lots of worried noises throughout, but I keep being super clear that we are all fine, and that we'll be home soon.

'Oh Gussy, please be careful. I know you think you're all grown up, but you aren't. Not really. You're my little boy and I don't want you to get caught up with whatever is going on with these people.'

Suddenly she gasps. 'Oh God, you haven't joined a cult, have you?'

This makes me laugh. What kind of cult would I even be interested in?

'No, I haven't joined a cult.'

'Good, because I hear deprogramming is expensive!' she jokes.

I didn't realise how much I missed her until I heard her voice and laugh.

'Don't worry, you won't have to deprogram me,' I laugh. 'But Mum, there's one more thing. Everyone here says they don't know who Jane is, but we think one or more of them are lying.'

'Why would they lie?'

'I have no idea, but I'm going to find out.'

'Please be careful. Look what happened last time you stuck your nose into a crime.'

'That worked out well in the end.'

'Maybe, but you were very lucky that it didn't go the other way. I want you to find Jane, I really do, but not if it's dangerous. Let the police handle it.'

It sounds like her and Kane have been talking, except they can't have been. I guess they both feel the same way about leaving things to the police.

'I promise I won't get into any trouble,' I say, which is not quite the same thing she was asking, but she seems to relax a little.

'Hmm, alright. My legs are a bit better now, by the way, thanks for asking,' she says, mock-seriously. I feel instantly guilty. I completely forgot why she wasn't here in the first place.

'Sorry! That's great.'

She chuckles. 'Anyway, I could probably come up there soon, if I continue improving. I'd like to help you figure this out.'

'I'm not sure when the roads will be open again. But I do need your help with this. I don't understand what's happening here. If Jane sent the message, then why get me to come here and not be here herself?'

She pauses for a moment. 'Maybe she's scared, or worried about what you might think of her and what she did back then? It's been such a long time. She might be afraid you'll reject her.'

I think about this for a moment. It does make sense.

'But if the message wasn't from her, then who sent it, and what do they want?'

'I wish I knew, Gussy.'

After I promise to keep Mum updated, we say goodbye. I can hear the end of Shell's and Kane's conversations with their parents. Once they're all over, we sit down together in the lounge room and debrief.

'Cheryl was all over the place,' Shell says. 'She'd called emergency services without even knowing what had happened. Typical. Everything's gotta be big!'

'Mum was a bit the same. But I think she had called Cheryl to see what she knew. And of course she was straight in next door to talk to your mum, Kane.'

Kane laughs. 'Yeah, I can imagine them both there, cracking a bottle of wine, making up theories about how our dead bodies were floating in the lake.'

The mention of dead bodies still makes me shiver a bit.

Shell clocks this and nudges him. 'Let's leave the dead body talk out of it, yeah?'

He glares at her, suddenly furious. 'You have to control everything, don't you? It's just a joke!' And with that, he marches into the bathroom and bangs the door shut.

Shell and I look at each other. 'Overreact much?' she says.

What's up with him? He was fine a minute ago and now he's having a tantrum in the bathroom. Nothing ever phases him much. I'm the crabby one, the anxious one. I hope he's okay. This is not like him at all, getting angry out of nowhere.

'He's probably just tired. The whole situation is a lot to take in,' I say feebly.

'Sure, it's a lot, but we're all going through it together, so he doesn't have to be a dick,' she replies.

'I guess we all deal with stress in different ways.'

She sighs. 'I guess that's true. How are you dealing with it?'

I don't know what to say. I'm not sure I am dealing with it at all. I know that I've been struggling with wanting to cut, and not wanting to lose all the progress I've made. I keep thinking about Walker, this handsome guy with everything going for him. Here one minute, then gone the next. And burnt like that, all twisted and black. The fire stole his life from under him.

I will never forget seeing his body on the jetty. It will haunt me for the rest of my life. And the smell . . .

I get up to go get a glass of water from the kitchen to distract me. Opening the cupboard, I see there's a photo taped face down to the inside of the door that totally wasn't there yesterday. I pull it off the tape and flip it over.

My stomach drops. It's a picture of Jane.

Chapter 24

Photo

I'm thrown for a minute but gather myself quickly. I march back into the loungeroom, calling over to the bathroom as I go. 'Kane, come and look at this photo I found in the kitchen!' I hold out the photo to Shell. 'It's Jane! She *has* been here. If they lied about her, what else are they all lying about?'

In this photo, she seems to be in a dark room without any obvious features. She is staring toward a patch of light, presumably coming from a window that's out of shot.

'This is a recent photo, too,' Shell says. She's right. Jane looks older here than in the pictures I have from the media, but you can totally see that they're the same person. The shape of her face is the same. The hair, her cheekbones, those sad eyes.

All of the photos I've seen of Jane are from about ten years ago. There were a few, but what stood out the most about her was that her eyes always looked so sad, so tired. And in this photo, I can still see that, like it never went away. I mean I want to think that she missed me and kept looking for me, but I don't really know what happened. The last we know is that she left Bellanta and was never heard from again.

It was like she disappeared, until now. Somewhere along the track she ended up here at The Circle. I've only known about her for a year and here I am, in the middle of nowhere, trying to find her. *Did she ever really try to look for me?* It's the question that created the hole in my stomach, the one I fill with food till it is overflowing and there's no room for any other feelings.

Kane has emerged from the bathroom, looking a little embarrassed. I'm too distracted to ask him what was up with his outburst. I show him the photo.

'Wow. Who could have put it here?'

I shake my head. 'I have to ask them. I need to know.'

Kane frowns. 'Actually, *how* could anyone have put that in here?'

'There's a bunch of keys for the cabins in Cath's place. They're not really hidden, just out in the open, and we've all been in and out of there so often that anyone could have borrowed a key without her noticing,' Shell says, drumming her fingers on her knee before turning to me. 'Why not ask Tobias? He seems to be the one you trust most.' I nod.

Kane lies down on the couch. 'Go for it. I'm staying here to get some more sleep.'

'Want me to come?' Shell asks.

I pause for a moment. 'No, I'm happy to go on my own,' I say.

* * *

I find Tobias moving the sandbags away from his door. He looks up as he hears me sludging in the mud. Nash's too-small shoes are rubbing uncomfortably, but at least my feet are dry.

'More questions, detective?' he says, smiling crookedly.

'Yes, a few.'

He stands up and puts the last sandbag down. 'Well, I was planning to go and see if the stones had sustained any damage from the storm, now that the rain has stopped. Come with me and I will answer your questions as we go. Sound fair?'

I nod.

He brushes his hands on his pants. 'Off we go then.'

I follow him up the hill to the stone circle. He starts examining the bases of the stones, making notes in a small, well-worn leather notebook. The surfaces of the stones are covered in splatters of mud. They look almost like oversized speckled eggs. Up close, they're not as mysterious as they seemed in the middle of the night, being bombarded by the storm.

I touch the surface of one, just lightly, almost expecting to get an electrical charge through my fingers. Nothing. It's cold, not red hot like it's channelling ancient power or possessed by aliens. Tobias must sense what I was hoping for.

'Just stones. Not magic,' he smiles and returns to his notebook.

They do have some form of power though. In the middle of this circle I can feel a strange energy, a calm flowing over me. But it's just a feeling, nothing tangible. I'm probably just enjoying being out in the fresh air, and not in our musty cabin.

He inspects some of the tufts of grass around the base of the stones. 'Nothing is displaced, and this grass is starting to dry already. I was worried the excess moisture might dislodge the stones, but it looks like everything is fine.'

'I have something I need to ask you.'

'One moment,' he says, scribbling away. Eventually he puts the notebook in his pocket and looks up. 'What was the question?'

'Yesterday no one said they knew Jane. But today I found a photo of her in our cabin. A recent photo.' I pull the picture out of my pocket and hand it to him.

He takes a good look and hands it back to me. I can't read his expression.

'Where did you find this, specifically?'

'It was taped inside one of the kitchen cupboards. And it wasn't there yesterday, I'm sure of it. Someone put it there. Was it you?'

He stares at me intently. I try to stare back but feel like I'm only looking at his patch, so I look over this shoulder a little instead.

'No, it was not me. I wonder who . . .' he says, almost to himself. Coming back to earth, he points at the photo. 'How do you feel about her?'

'Huh?'

'I am just curious. Did you come here to reconnect with your mother, or to confront her?'

I stare at my feet. I don't really know. A bit of both? It's none of his business.

'I just want to meet her,' I say, looking back up at him. He smiles. Suddenly his phone rings.

'I have to get this, it's the police.' He puts his phone to one ear, listening. 'Hello, Detective Carland. Thank you for getting back to me. We have a situation here . . . you got my message? Yes, okay, yes.'

He puts his hand over the mouthpiece. 'Get the others to meet us at Cath's.'

Fifteen minutes later, everyone is sitting in Cath's cabin *again*. She is making tea and toast for us *again*. It's like one of those *Doctor Who* episodes where they are trapped in a time loop, repeating the same cycle over and over.

Tobias is updating everyone on a call he had with the detective.

'I just spoke to Detective Carland. He said that the flooding is definitely going down, and they should be able to get through to us in the morning.'

He looks at everyone, waiting for a response. We're all quiet. Maybe it's all starting to get real now. The implications of a body and some kind of investigation are starting to hit. It's kind of exciting.

Tobias continues with his announcement. 'For now, we have been asked to wait for the police and emergency services. I told them we still have power thanks to the generator, and that we are okay for food for a few days.'

'What will the police do when they get here?' Cath asks. She looks tired, pulling at yet another thread on her jumper. At the rate she's going, she's going to unspool it entirely.

'Interview us, I presume. Examine the body and the houseboat and see if they can figure out what happened. We are to go nowhere until they get here.'

'Where would we go with the roads flooded?' laughs Cath humourlessly.

'We could escape by boat,' says Nash, 'but there are none, except Walker's burnt-out coffin.'

'Nash, stop it!' snaps Cath. She seems to be really losing her cool. I guess it's starting to take its toll out on all of us, but he's quite a negative person. Looking after this lot, especially needy Greta, would drain the patience out of anyone.

'What do we do in the meantime?' asks Shell.

Tobias is firm. 'It means that it is time for you kids to stop playing games and wait for the professionals to get here.'

Shell stands up, bristling. 'There's no need to be so patronising. We aren't playing games. We've solved a crime before. We're trying to find out what happened, and what all of this has to do with Gus's mother. It's incredibly serious.'

Tobias seems impressed.

Shell has inspired me. The photo of Jane is still in my pocket. I think I might try and push this a bit and see what happens. It looks like our investigation into Walker's murder might be done soon. Time to get back to the case we actually came here to solve.

I take the photo out of my pocket. 'If anyone is playing games it's one of you. I found this photo of my mother taped inside the cupboard. A recent photo. She's been here, or someone here knows her, at least. But you all told me you'd never seen her.'

I hold up the photo for everyone to see clearly.

There is silence around the room. A few furtive glances pass between Maxine and Greta, and Cath and Tobias. Nash doesn't even bother to look up.

'I have already told Gus that I did not put it there,' Tobias says to the group.

No one else responds.

Shell stands next to me, and Kane stands on the other side of me. We must look like a superhero movie poster.

'Seriously? One of you must have put it there, because it wasn't there when we arrived.'

I stare at each one of them in turn, trying to shame someone into saying something.

Greta shakes her head. 'I didn't put it there.'

Maxine nods her agreement. 'Me neither.'

Cath and Nash say nothing.

'Argh!' I shout in frustration. I've had enough. I stomp out of the cabin, Kane and Shell hot on my heels. I can't be around these liars any longer.

* * *

We hole up in our cabin for the rest of the afternoon. I'm stewing in anger over the fact that someone has dropped half of a clue in my lap but won't tell me the whole story. I try to distract myself with a book and a podcast, but my mind is doing somersaults, rolling wildly from one scenario to another. I feel like I'm so close to figuring this all out, but someone is holding onto the final piece of the puzzle. It's like the answer is being dangled in front of me, but each time I stretch out my arms, it moves away, just out of reach.

At around 7 pm there's a knock on the door. We look up and see a shape through the ribbed glass, then they are gone again. We look at each other, confused. Kane gets up and opens the door. There's a big glass container sitting on the doorstep, covered in silver foil.

'Pasta,' he says, putting it on the kitchen bench and peeling back the foil. 'Still hot.'

'Cath must have done this to stop us from coming over tonight and causing another scene,' Shell says.

'A hundred per cent,' says Kane.

'Works for me. I cannot spend another minute sitting in that room with those people right now,' I mutter.

Shell's inspecting the pasta. 'It actually looks good. I'll dish it up now.' She goes into the kitchen and grabs some plates and then gets some forks from the cutlery drawer. 'Weird, there's forks and spoons but no knives,' she says. I look at Kane but he's staring straight ahead, avoiding my eyes.

We chow down the pasta.

'Let's talk about something other than this murder for a change,' I say. I need to get out of my own churning head. The last couple of days are spiking my anxiety, even though I've been taking my meds.

'Will you be back playing footy soon?' I ask Kane between mouthfuls.

He stretches his leg out. 'Not quite. My knee is fine, but not strong enough for full-on training. I've had to miss this season. Defo tracking for next season though.'

'Any luck with the job hunting?' Shell asks.

He shakes his head.

'Would you come back and finish high school?' I ask.

'Never! Knowing my luck, I'd end up in a class with you losers!' He grins at me.

'Ever thought of security work?' Shell asks, cracking her knuckles for emphasis.

He raises his eyebrows. 'No, but that's a good idea. All you have to do is be able to stand your ground and look mean.'

'Well, you have the skills for that,' Shell laughs. 'One of my dad's clients is a big security firm. Maybe I could find out if they're hiring?'

He sits up enthusiastically. 'That would be awesome, thanks. Would I have a gun?'

'No, but you'd have a uniform and maybe one of those big walkie talkies like police have.'

He gives her a thumbs up.

'That's a great suggestion, Shell,' I say. It's really nice of her, especially since they don't always get on.

'What about you? What are you gonna do after you finish school? Uni?'

She smiles. 'I'm going to study law.'

'So Gus will join the police and be a cop catching criminals, and you'll be in court defending them?' Kane laughs.

Shell shakes her head. 'I'm thinking about environmental law actually. Looking at how people work with the environmental policies and rules and things like that.'

'Like stuff to do with climate change?'

'Yes. We have to stop burning fossil fuels before time runs out. Laws and polices can support the change that is needed.'

Kane stretches his leg again and says, almost under his breath. 'You two are way smarter than me.'

'Maybe in some ways,' I smile. 'But it's not like you're stupid, Kane. You just focus more on the physical stuff than the mental stuff.'

I mean it as a compliment, but he looks unsure how to take it.

After we eat, I realise I'm exhausted, so I say goodnight and head to bed early. Instead of going to sleep, I lie awake in bed and think about the photo of Jane, and where she might be.

Being this close to finding Jane and hitting this wall – it hurts. I got lots of answers last year, but every answer slips another question through the door as it closes.

I'm so glad I have friends like Shell and Kane, who have my back and watch out for me as I go through my weirdness and my anxiety. Last year was a lot. And I'm still figuring out where I fit in the world, even knowing what I do now.

Shell knocks on the door before coming in and sitting on her side of the bed. I feel it dip with her weight.

'You okay?'

'Mostly, yeah,' I say. 'Just a bit overwhelmed. And angry at the others for what they're not telling me.'

'Yeah, it's cruel. I'm sorry that we're still no closer to Jane. And that the police will get through tomorrow and our investigation will be over.'

'Thanks. Still, it'd be good if our detective agency could solve it first, wouldn't it?' I say.

Shell laughs. 'Yes, with or without the others' help.'

Chapter 25

Vial

That night I have the weirdest dreams. One is about being a boy in the corner of a room. Jane is waving a magic purple scarf across my face and back. She waves it in front of the goldfish bowl on a table. When she lifts the scarf, the bowl is gone.

I clap my hands. Jane places the scarf over my head. Through the gauze, I can still see her in the centre of swirling eddies of magic. Suddenly it goes quiet. When I take the scarf off my head, she's gone.

Silence.

I put the scarf over my head again. In this gauzy world I feel safer.

Abracadabra! I say. But nothing happens. I stay exactly where I am.

I wake up sweating, my heart pounding.

Shell snores next to me. I want to ask her what to do next, but I don't want to wake her. She always knows what to do.

Maybe I could talk to Kane. I can't get to sleep with my mind spinning off its axis like this. I'm scratching my cuts again and keep thinking about the knife I took from Greta's house today.

I quietly lift the blankets up and put my feet on the floor, making sure that Shell is still asleep. Then I pull my T-shirt down to properly cover my belly and pull on my jeans. The shape of the box cutter sticks out at me, but I put my hand on it anyway to make sure it's really there. It feels cold, even through the denim. I feel calm already just touching it. The dream is stuck in my head, making me hot and sweaty and panicky.

I can't believe I stole a knife. Putting my hand over my pocket in case Kane is awake when I go into the lounge to the bathroom, I tiptoe through the door and peer through the gloom, trying to see if Kane's asleep or awake. But he's not there.

The couch is empty.

He's not in the kitchen. I check the bathroom but it's empty too. I go to the front window but I can't see him. Grabbing a jacket from the hooks by the door, I pick up the red torch and walk out into the cold night. I do a lap of the cabin, but there's no sight of him. I'm about to start calling his name when I see something in the middle of the stone circle. It seems to be a figure, lit up by the moonlight somehow.

It's Kane.

What's he doing? I head up the hill as fast as I can. As I get closer, I realise that Kane is running around the inside of the circle.

'Kane!' I call out. But he doesn't respond. I call out again. I'm close enough that he must be able to hear me, but he doesn't even look my way. He just keeps running, round and round. Laps, like he's in training. Something is super wrong here.

'Kane, what's going on?' I'm standing just outside the circle now, but still no response, no recognition that I'm here at all. His eyes are creeping me out. They're open very wide and don't seem to be blinking.

'*Kane!*' I'm yelling now. Is he sleepwalking? Or sleep running? Is that even a thing? I'm trying to remember what I've seen on TV about dealing with sleepwalkers. I think you're supposed to gently coax them awake. Here goes nothing.

'Kane, it's time to come back to the cabin,' I say. No response.

Here goes nothing. 'Bro!' Gym guys all call each other 'bro' right?

Is that a thing? It's not like I've ever stepped foot in a gym myself. 'Hey, bro!'

He turns his head and looks at me, but it's as if he can see through me, like I'm a ghost or something. He starts to slow down to a walk, but he's still pacing around the circle. I can't believe the gym speak is working.

'Time to finish your set, bro,' I say.

He stops walking. He just stands still, looking right at me, his eyes big and unblinking.

'Come this way,' I say, gently guiding his arm. He moves a little. I start to lead him out of the circle and back to the cabin. He doesn't say anything. He's sweating from the running, but also cold to the touch. How long has he been out here?

Slowly we make our way down the hill toward the cabin. He still doesn't say anything. Just stares and walks at my pace. In a few minutes I'm guiding him back through the door and over to the couch. I put my hand on his shoulder to push him down into a sitting position. He's like a shop window dummy, clumsy but malleable. After a few false starts I manage to get him to lie down.

Once he's down, I cover him up with the blanket. It was so cold outside . . . I find another blanket in the cupboard and put that on him too. Maybe I should put a jacket over him as well?

I notice his sports bag poking out from under the couch and suddenly remember that he took my knife. Now is the perfect opportunity to get it back. I quietly rummage through his bag looking for its familiar green handle but instead I find a vial of some liquid and a box of needles. *What the . . . ?*

The label on the vial says 'Decclarobol'. Never heard of it. Shit, I hope he doesn't have something wrong with him. He's never mentioned anything. But that's very him, to not say anything and just keep being the cheery person in the room.

I grab my phone and google the name of the medication. My heart drops when the results pop up. It's an anabolic steroid. I can't believe it. This is dangerous stuff.

Is this why he wants a collab, someone to sponsor his posts? To pay for steroids? Things are worse than I thought. And of course I've been too wrapped up in my own head to see what was going on right in front of my eyes.

I note that the website I googled says there are lots of side effects to using steroids, including sleepwalking and mood swings. It explains so much, but I still have so many questions.

Chapter 26

Pyro

The next morning I wonder if suddenly tea and toast are going to appear on the doorstep, like last night's dinner. I'm disappointed when nothing materialises.

Shell washes and dries the container the pasta came in. Together, we head over to Cath's again. I'm not looking forward to it, after yesterday, but we don't really have a choice since there's no food at our cabin.

Shell plays the diplomat for us. As Cath answers the door, she thanks her for last night's dinner and holds out the clean container. Cath takes it with a curt nod. 'I think we all needed a night off.' She eyes me carefully and then ushers us in.

As we sit on the couch again – our usual spots – she puts some bread in the toaster.

There are so many things in my head that I want to talk to this lot about. I'm still angry after yesterday, but I don't want to piss anyone off. Plus I'm super hungry, so I'm not going to say anything until I've had breakfast. Food first, questions second.

For whatever reason, the others all seem to gravitate to her cabin too, and by mid-morning, everyone is here again. Even Nash has left the sanctity of his room to eat.

I lean over to Shell and whisper, 'I need to pick up that conversation, but what do I say?'

Shell whispers back. 'Maybe we could move things along in a different way? See where that gets us?'

I nod. 'Sure. What do you have in mind?'

She smiles innocently at me. 'I want to throw a bomb and see who reacts.'

'This should be good,' says Kane, not wanting to be left out of the whispering.

Shell grins and hauls herself to her feet. She paces around a little, then stands directly in the middle of the room and faces everyone.

In a clear, controlled voice, she begins. 'Which one of you started the fire?'

For a moment no one moves or says anything. Cath gives Shell a death stare. Fortunately, this is Shell's superpower, and she gives as good as she gets.

'Someone is dead and you're all hiding something,' Shell says without breaking eye contact.

Cath breaks first and looks away. 'You are really getting on my nerves.'

Shell points at Cath. 'I think you know who did it. But you won't say. I think you're protecting someone. One of you or all of you.'

Everyone just stares at her, saying nothing. But Greta seems particularly uneasy, looking around at the others.

Shell turns toward Greta. 'Was it you? Did you light the fire?'

Greta shakes her head furiously. 'No, it wasn't me. Stop looking at me like that.'

'Then who was it?' Shell pushes.

Greta looks panicked, like a wild animal backed into a corner. 'It wasn't me. It was him. He's a pyromaniac!' she yells, pointing at Nash.

The minute the words leave her mouth, Greta's face warps in horror. She slaps her hand up to cover her mouth as if to push the words back in and looks up at Cath, tears forming in her eyes.

Cath shakes her head and sits down, sighing. 'Oh Greta.'

'I'm sorry, it just jumped out.'

Cath seems to be taking a minute to ponder something, her brows furrowing. Eventually she takes a deep breath. 'We moved up here because Nash had lit fires at his last two schools.'

Shell, Kane and I look at each other in disbelief. Everyone else's heads whip around in Nash's direction.

'Bitch!' Nash snaps at Greta, his face a violent red. He leaps to his feet and stomps out of the front door of the cabin, banging the door behind him so hard I'm surprised that the glass doesn't crack. Several of the jackets by the door fall off their hooks with the impact.

Cath runs her hand through her hair. 'I wish . . . it's not his fault. It's a medical disorder. He struggles with impulse control.'

'He makes me mad when he gets you in trouble,' Greta says, eyes downcast, tears falling silently down her cheeks.

'Hold on. Nash is a firebug? And you didn't think to mention it?' Maxine snaps angrily at Cath. There's a whiff of self-righteous indignation in her tone. I bet this is something she almost never gets to express with someone as strong as Cath.

Tobias gets to his feet, fuming. 'A fire kills someone, and there is a pyromaniac among us, and yet you said nothing, Cath?' His usually deep voice is high with fury and there's a hardness to his jawline that I haven't seen before. Even when he was trading barbs with Walker, he sounded in control, but that seems to have been stamped out now by sheer anger.

Cath winces and holds out her hands in an almost pleading manner. 'He hasn't lit a fire since we got here. I brought him here to protect him from his worst tendencies. And it's worked.'

'Until now,' mutters Greta.

Cath turns to Greta abruptly. 'Stop it! He didn't do this. He's better now, I'm sure of it.'

Greta recoils with a stunned look. It's like she's surprised that Cath could turn on her like that.

'If you're so sure, then why didn't you mention that he likes lighting fires before? We found him there by the houseboat that night, staring at the fire,' says Shell.

Cath's full beam glare turns on Shell. 'My son's illness is none of your business.'

'You'll have to tell the police,' Kane says.

Cath rounds on him. 'You kids can't tell me what to do about my own son.'

I suddenly feel sorry for Nash. Everyone's talking about him and he's not here to defend himself. I get up and walk out of the cabin. I can't see Nash, but I hear the sound of a motor revving and suddenly the quad bike we saw earlier comes screeching into view with Nash virtually standing up in the seat, one hand on the handlebars.

He's yelling something at the top of his voice. I don't think it's words, but more of a battle cry. He looks furious and his face is deeply red.

He speeds the bike up really close to me. I stand still, frozen in place, wondering if he's actually going to knock me down. At the last minute, he swerves away and splashes me with a light spray of mud. Then he takes off and does whatever the opposite of a lap of honour is around the cabins.

Cath and the others all come out to see what the commotion is. Cath looks exhausted as she watches her angry son burn around the place, the four massive wheels sending mud flying everywhere. It looks like she is going to say something, but then she seems to stop. Maybe she feels it's better that he gets it out of his system? She shakes her head and then walks over to the garden and disappears from sight.

Nash is looping back toward us when he sees Greta peering out of Cath's cabin door. He revs the engine even harder and raises the front wheels up, like a horse about to charge. Greta darts back inside instantly.

I remember feeling that kind of anger once. A few wheelies on a quad bike wouldn't have been enough to calm me down back then, and I doubt it's enough to help Nash now.

Eventually everyone grows tired of the show, returning indoors. Nash seems to have lost steam as well, driving the bike back into the garage. Later I find him, out in the front yard, throwing muddy rocks at the sign by the road. He seems like a little kid now, not a snarky nineteen-year-old.

'You okay?' I ask.

He turns and looks at me in surprise.

'What do you want?' he mutters.

'Got kinda intense in there . . . and out here,' I venture.

He doesn't respond and just throws a fistful of mud. He hits the sign this time with a satisfying squelching sound. 'Score!' he shouts, pumping his fist to the air.

'Nice one,' I say.

He looks at me again. 'Are they all in there saying I set the houseboat on fire and killed him?'

I shake my head. 'No, your mum is saying that you haven't lit a fire since you got here. Mostly they're upset that they didn't know about your . . . past . . . before now.'

'They'll just assume I did it. Especially that little freak.'

He and Greta must really hate each other.

'She wishes I was gone so she could be Mum's only kid.'

'Why?'

'Mum took her in when we moved down here. She's been in and out of care homes, never had a real family before, I guess. She's obsessed with Mum.'

I guess Greta feels like she owes Cath a lot.

'Well, if you didn't do it, then who did?'

He looks back at me. 'Dunno. All I know is that there's less chance than ever of me getting out of here now he's gone.'

'You want to go that bad?'

He's back throwing rocks. 'Yeah. Sick of that little creep, and this place. I need to get out of here even more now that the drunk and the professor know. They'll be judging me. I wanna have a life of my own.'

I know the feeling. I wouldn't want to be trapped here with these people either.

'Then why were you throwing sand at Walker like a kid? Wouldn't you be better off being nice to him? Sounds like he was the answer to your problem.'

'I know, but he was such a dick. I hated him.'

'I get that. But even if your mum doesn't sell this place, why couldn't you just leave anyway?'

He glares at me and throws another rock, apparently ignoring me. I guess that's a sticky question. Maybe he doesn't know? Maybe he's scared?

I want to help him somehow, which is mad given that he's a potential murderer. But I want to believe him.

'So, why do you light fires?' I ask carefully, fully prepared to get blasted.

He just shrugs. 'The shrink said I'm angry 'cos dad left and I got bullied at school. He said it's my way of taking control back. Or some shit like that.'

Wow. I didn't expect him to answer so honestly.

I wonder if he has a police record. That would make it hard to get a job. Maybe that's why he's here when he doesn't want to be. It would explain his aggressive attitude.

I look out down the hill to the lake. The burnt houseboat is still sitting there, like a cancer on the water. I can see a figure standing on the jetty. It's Cath. She seems to be laying some flowers, from the garden I guess, on the water by the houseboat. That's nice. She clearly liked him, despite everything. I watch her let them float away.

I look back at Nash. I can believe he's a firebug, but it's kind of ironic that the most likely suspect just explained he's also the one with the least motive.

But if he didn't do it, who did? And was it just to kill Walker, or was it to save the community, or even the stone circle? Was it all of the above? Or are we missing some vital clue that will help all the pieces of the puzzle fall into place?

Chapter 27

Timeline

Kane, Shell and I walk up to the stone circle now that the sun is out. Anything to avoid going back to the cabin again.

'I asked Greta that question thinking it might provoke something, but I totally didn't expect her to tell everyone that Nash is a pyro. Did not see that coming,' Shell says, looking quietly pleased with herself.

'You'd make a great court lawyer if you decide to go beyond environmental law one day,' I say.

She smiles as she slowly walks around the circle.

Kane leans against one of the stones, his hands behind his head. 'Now we know he's a pyro, everything makes sense. I kept wondering why he was down by the houseboat just standing there like he was hypnotised.'

I feel the way Kane just lolls on the stone is somehow disrespectful to the circle, but I think it's too strange to say anything.

'Just because he's lit fires in the past doesn't mean he lit this one,' I say. I know this sounds pretty flimsy, but I think I believe Nash.

'No, but it makes him a *major* suspect,' says Shell. She's kicking the grass around the base of the stones. Despite the rain, it looks brittle and dry.

I just don't see it. 'He doesn't have a motive. He wants Cath to sell up and get out of here, so hurting Walker has the opposite effect.'

I stand on the flat keystone Tobias mentioned, in the middle of the circle, and try to clear my head. Could he really have done it? 'His moods are up and down, like he's got no self-control at all. Maybe he just lost it? He hated Walker so much that he just cracked and set the houseboat on fire?'

Shell agrees. 'He's a loose cannon, sure. But what set him off in particular?'

I shake my head. Shell moves off and wanders away from the circle, toward the garage.

Speaking of moods being up and down . . . I turn my attention to Kane.

'We need to talk about last night. I found you outside, running around the circle in your sleep. It was terrifying. Since when do you sleepwalk?'

'What do you mean?' He stands up straight, looking sheepishly at me.

'You know you do this, right? Or was last night the first time?'

He blushes and looks at his feet, shuffling on the spot. 'Not sure really. Dad caught me a few months back, so that's the first I knew about it.'

'What were you doing when he found you?'

Kane grins up at me. 'Lifting bricks like they were weights in the yard, at like 2 am. Dedication!'

'It's not a joke,' I say.

The cocky smile disappears from his face. 'Mum and Dad are worried that I'll do something dangerous while I'm asleep and not even know.' It's so rare to see him vulnerable, the whole alpha male thing falling off like a snake shedding its skin. He really does look scared.

'What if I walked in front of a car or something?' He rubs his hands together nervously.

'You're such a muscle bro now that you'd wreck the car, not the other way round,' I laugh.

'True,' he smiles. He seems relieved that I'm not pushing him to say more.

'Do you want me to tie you to the couch at night so you can't leave?'

'Kinky!'

We both laugh, avoiding the serious thing in front of us, like we usually do.

I remember when we were growing up, if we had a disagreement or argument over something, we could figure it out by watching *Doctor Who*, our one shared thing. By the time the end theme music is playing, whatever we were arguing about has dissipated into the air and everything is cool again.

I need to talk to him about the steroids and needles too. But before I can say anything, Shell comes back, her phone in her hand.

'Let's take another look at the timeline, now that we've learned a bit more,' she says, doing another lap of the circle. 'We should compare people's movements and see how likely it is one of them did it versus the other. We can solve this ourselves. I've got the timeline here,' she says, holding up her phone.

Timeline

3.15 pm we arrive

3.30 pm Walker arrives

3.45 pm Walker leaves

4.00 pm sandbagging

4.45 pm we finish sandbagging and set up cabin six

5.30 pm Shell goes to cabin one, Greta already there. Gus and Kane go to cabin five to see Tobias. Cath is in garden, Nash in room? Maxine getting ready

5.45 pm sunset

5.50 pm Maxine arrives at cabin one

5.55 pm Gus and Kane leave cabin five and arrive at cabin one

6.25 pm Tobias hears boom. Explosion?

6.30 pm Tobias arrives at cabin one

6.40 pm Nash sneaks out of cabin one

6.45 pm Shell sees the fire

The timeline looks almost the same as it did before our interviews. It's not super helpful. We need to work out a way to separate legitimate suspects from people with solid alibis.

'We need to go through each suspect like the police would,' I say. 'Let's start by looking at motive and opportunity.'

'That's what I was thinking. We should start with the people with the weakest alibis,' says Shell, enthusiastically bobbing her head.

'Cath says she was in the garden, but we have no way of knowing if that's true, since no one saw her,' I say.

'Okay, so she had opportunity. What's her motive?' Shell asks, tapping into her phone.

'Walker wanted her to sell, but she didn't want to. As she said herself, no matter what pressure he put on her, she could just say no. But now we know she also came here to keep Nash from lighting fires.'

'Plus she and Walker were seeing each other, don't forget,' Kane adds.

'Brutal way to break up with someone,' says Shell with a half-smile. 'But if she did it, I can't think what she gets out of it.'

I feel like there could be something here, like one of the threads Cath keeps pulling from her jumper. 'What if . . . what if he was blackmailing her over Nash?'

Shell frowns. 'Maybe. But only Greta seemed to know his secret.'

'Maybe she knew he'd be on the houseboat and she went down there to get naked with him or something, and he was up to something, so she set the fire?' Kane says, snorting.

Shell grimaces. 'It's all about sex with you isn't it? You think that just because you're okay with sexualising yourself that everyone else is into it too!'

'Woah, I was just joking.' Kane steps back in surprise, looking a bit hurt.

Shell's mouth is open like she can't quite believe what she's said. She looks down. 'Sorry, it's just a bit tedious.'

He grins and flexes his arms. 'Are you secretly into me and jealous of all my followers?' he jokes.

She makes a mock gagging sound.

We think in silence for a bit, with just the sound of the wind rustling through the trees.

'What if it was an accident?' asks Kane, scratching his head.

'I don't know about that,' I say. 'Tobias seemed totally convinced that the fire was set intentionally. Remember he found that weird gizmo on the houseboat?'

Kane raises his hand in a *hold up* kind of gesture. 'Hear me out,' he says. 'I think the fire was intentional, but what if the murder was an accident? What if no one expected him to be there and they were just setting his houseboat on fire to send him a message?'

'Like what, a warning?' asks Shell.

'Yeah, like *stop hooking up with my mother*,' Kane adds. Shell gives him the death glare. 'C'mon, I'm serious. Nash is so sketchy. I mean, we can't deny the pyromaniac thing and him staring at the fire like he was possessed.'

Shell looks at her phone. 'Yeah, you're right. He said he was out packing sandbags at 5, but wouldn't he have been done by then? We finished our sandbagging at 4.45, and we were the last ones done. It's not much of an alibi. Cath said he was in his room at the party, but Greta wasn't sure.'

'Okay, so he had the opportunity. But I still don't see his motive. He may have hated Walker but he wanted to leave here. He was hoping Cath would sell up so he could be free.'

Kane smirks. 'Has he lit a fire in you or something, Goose?'

I can feel myself blushing.

'Anyway, that's not the only motive,' Kane says. 'He's a pyro. He loves to set fires, and he can't control it. Simple.'

Shell nods. 'But I'm confused about the trigger. Cath said he hasn't lit a fire since he's been here. Can we trust her?'

I think about the fact that someone planted that photo of Jane in our cabin. 'Can we trust *any* of them? They seem to be good at sticking together to cover things up. Like who is this John dude? He may have a connection to Jane. Plus, who put that photo of Jane in our cabin? None of them responded to that, other than Tobias. At least one of them is lying about that alone.'

I feel like the lying about the photo and the murder of Walker are all connected – but how?

'A hundred per cent. We can't trust *any* of them,' Kane agrees.

'I trust Tobias more than the others,' I say.

Shell frowns. 'I can't put my finger on it, but all I know is he's lying about something.'

I want her to be wrong, but she's usually right about these things. It's annoying and reassuring at the same time. Still, that doesn't make him a killer.

'I feel the same way about Greta. There's something not right there,' I counter.

'Look, she's a bit nervy, that's all,' says Shell. 'Given your anxiety

Gus, I would have thought you'd feel a bit more empathy for her. She means no harm.'

Ouch. She's right. I should be a little bit more understanding. But there's something that just irks me about her.

'You're right, as always. Sorry. We should still go through her timeline though. Where was she at 5.30 and 6?'

'I was with her in the house from 5.30, helping with those sad decorations and setting out snacks.'

'The whole time?' I ask.

Shell nods. 'Yes. She never left, so she couldn't have done it.'

'Okay, no opportunity, but big motive. She clearly loves Cath and doesn't want her to sell and lose her home and her community, so she's got a lot to lose,' I say.

'Is that enough of a motive for her to overcome her fears? She was afraid of going out in the storm, remember?' says Kane.

'It's pretty unlikely that she would have headed off in the storm to burn the houseboat if she's scared of lightning,' I agree. 'But she's also oddly attached to the stone circle. I think she thinks it has powers. She's talked about it being special, in almost a religious way. And I get that – it has a quality that is hard to ignore.'

'I admit that she's suspicious, but she was with me. So how could she have done it?'

'How sure of those times can we be? I mean, Tobias isn't an expert or whatever,' Kane says.

'I've thought about that too. We only have his word for those times. He could be covering up his own tracks,' Shell says.

I rub my chin. 'Good point.'

We're all silent for a minute.

'Maybe we should leave it to the police,' says Kane. 'They can figure this out way easier. They'll have forensics and everything. We should leave it to the professionals.' He starts to walk away from the circle.

'It worked out okay last time we investigated a crime,' I say.

'You nearly drowned!' he barks back.

'Okay, sorry, I know what you mean. But doesn't some part of you want to solve this before the police do?'

A smile comes over his face. 'Yes, a bit, but not as much as you two do. Why don't you try to focus on what we actually came here for?'

'I'm trying. I swear there's something that links them all and I just can't figure it out. I feel like the answer is right here, in the back of my brain, but I'm too slow to put it all together.'

Shell scrolls the timeline on her phone. 'Let's keep going for now. We have Cath who was in the garden but no one saw her. Opportunity, but no motive. Nash was missing for a while and was found near the fire. Opportunity, but not enough motive, unless we just blame pyromania in general. Greta was with me. Big motive, but no opportunity. That's zero for three, which leaves Maxine and Tobias.'

Kane gets out his phone this time. 'We know Maxine is a bit of a drunk so she's probably unreliable. She says she was getting ready between 5.30 and close to 6, but no one saw her either.'

'Enjoying too much wine doesn't mean she's a murderer,' I say. 'But then Greta mentioned seeing her digging in the garden with a pitchfork . . . we still have to look into that,' I remind them.

Shell nods and makes a note. 'Okay, so she had opportunity. But what's her motive? Walker certainly knew about her past, and her daughter. Maybe that was the first time she discovered he knew about it and she just lost it?'

'What if he was blackmailing her?' Kane suggests.

'What's with you guys and blackmail?' Shell laughs. 'And what would he blackmail her for? He was rich and she lives here in a shitty cabin. I doubt she's hiding millions under her mattress.'

'What if it was just anger?' Kane counters. 'She was furious that he discussed her secrets in front of everyone?'

'Okay,' says Shell. 'You're saying that maybe there was more, like that was just the tip of the iceberg of secrets?'

Sounds plausible. I mean it's hard to know what other secrets there would be, but that's the nature of secrets really. They expand in the dark. And the more you try to hide them, the more lies you have to tell.

'She's also quite protective of Greta, so maybe she did it because Walker came after her,' suggests Kane.

'Seems excessive,' I say.

'Maybe that's why she stayed behind that night with Greta, to stop her from seeing the dead body, because she knew what we'd find?' Shell says thoughtfully.

'I think she stayed behind just because she was drunk. If she went down to the jetty, she would have fallen in,' Kane chuckles.

'I can't help thinking that Walker knowing about her past is significant,' I say. 'Do you think Walker was digging up dirt on all of them to make them sell? Or did Cath tell him?'

'Good point,' Shell says. 'For now, Maxine has motive *and* opportunity. She goes up to the top of the suspect list.'

'Which just leaves the professor,' says Kane.

I really don't want it to be Tobias. I trust him, for some reason.

I sigh. 'Kane and I left him at his cabin at about 5.55 but he didn't show up at the party until closer to 6.30. He said he was doing revisions to his book and lost track of time. Seems quite likely, given who he is. But it means that there are no witnesses.'

'And it means he had the opportunity,' Shell says. 'And he's the one giving us the timing, so he could be lying to cover himself.'

She's right. I have to consider him as a suspect. 'Remember how he just tore Walker a new one the other day? He can be pretty ruthless when he wants to be. I wouldn't want to cross him.'

'But what's his motive? To protect the stone circle?' Kane asks.

'Yes, but it sounds like he had applied to get a heritage overlay on the circle, so it will be protected soon anyway,' I say.

'Does he have any other motive?' Shell asks.

'Walker did hint at knowing something secret about Tobias too. Maybe it was something that could make him lose his job, or his research funding?' I suggest.

'Sure, but like what?' asks Shell. 'Embezzlement? Inappropriate behaviour with a student?'

'Now who's sexualising everything!' snarks Kane.

Shell rolls her eyes at him and types what we've discussed into her Notes app. 'Tobias has opportunity, and motive, kinda.'

'Right, so that's two people without a motive and one person without opportunity. Therefore, Maxine or Tobias are our best bets,' I say, heart sinking.

'What do we do now?' Kane asks.

'We need to find some evidence, one way or another.'

Chapter 28

Watch

At around midday, there's a knock at our cabin door. Shell answers and lets Tobias in to the main room. He sits next to me on the couch with a sigh. He looks worried, and his patch is a little askew.

'There has been a . . . *development*. I need to ask you all a question, and I need you to be completely honest with me. You will not get into trouble.'

He looks at each of us in turn, talking slowly and carefully like he's giving a tutorial about something complex to vacuous kids.

'What's happened?' asks Shell.

He leans back into the couch. 'Did one of you take Simon Walker's watch?'

'It's missing?' I say in surprise. *How?*

Tobias looks at me first, the question unsaid. 'It wasn't me.'

Shell and Kane shake their heads as Tobias looks at them in turn.

'I didn't.'

'Me either.'

Shell's voice drops a little. 'When did you last see it?'

Tobias rubs his hands together. 'I don't really know. It was there when I put him in the spare room. But then I put a sheet over him completely, so his arms were not visible. It could have been taken yesterday, it could have been taken an hour ago. I do not know.'

'Why would someone flog his watch? How much is it worth?' Kane asks.

Tobias takes his phone out of his pocket and taps in his passcode, which is hilariously boomer: 6-5-4-3-2-1.

He googles something then shows me his screen. 'It's a NASA Jupiter Astronaut's watch, worth around $20,000.'

'Whoa, who wears a watch worth twenty k?' asks Kane.

'A showy salesman with a rich father,' says Tobias dryly.

I start to think out loud. 'The killer and the thief must be two different people. I mean, the killer would have just taken the watch on the night of the murder. Why wait until later on when you might be caught taking it?'

Tobias stands up and moves toward the window. 'Not necessarily. The identity of the thief and the killer could be the same. The killer may have set the fire but had to leave Walker there, so they would not have gotten a chance to take it then. They may have come back for it later.'

'Hang on. Why didn't the watch burn?' I ask.

'It is made of pure titanium with a diamond crystal face. It is literally designed to survive a rocket blowing up.'

'But would the thief know that?' Shell asks.

'Walker had boasted about that watch more than once. I knew the make and model by heart, and I know nothing about watches. Anyone could have looked it up to see how much it was worth.'

'Do we need to do a house-to-house search again?' asks Kane, a little too enthusiastically. 'Turn each place over? It's gotta still be here, but once the roads are open, the thief could leave and take it with them.'

Shell is up now, pacing as she always does when she's onto something. 'The watch can't be the reason he was killed. But it might be a symbol.'

Tobias smiles at her. 'Well, yes, it could be a symbol of what a flashy idiot he was. Taking it would be a way to really insult him.'

Someone has been killed and it can't have been for a watch. No one's that nuts. *Or are they?*

Chapter 29

Tape

The noise of a large vehicle braking in the distance cracks the silence. Through the front window, I see a big white Toyota Land Cruiser with the blue police checker pattern around the sides, and a massive bull bar on the front, has pulled up outside Cath's cabin.

The police are here!

Even though this means we'll have to end our investigation, a part of me is excited. I want to watch what they do, every step. I've wanted to join the police for years and now I'm about to get a free training session for when I sit the police exam.

'Finally,' says Tobias, putting his phone back into his jacket pocket.

We walk down toward cabin one. Cath reaches the police car first, with Greta not far behind. There's no sign of Maxine or Nash.

Two uniformed officers step out. The first is a middle-aged woman, lean and fit looking, with mousy blonde hair in a short, efficient ponytail. The other is a really built young guy, tall and broad, with big bushy eyebrows and a five o'clock shadow. They both have semi-automatic weapons holstered to them, as well as tasers. Real cops!

The ponytailed cop walks forward to Cath, and holds out her hand. 'I'm Senior Constable Katrina Sutton. And this is my colleague, Constable Nick Couttas. I'm glad we finally got through to you.'

Cath shakes her hand and nods to Constable Couttas.

'Now, let's see this body we've been hearing about.'

Senior Constable Sutton's eyes move toward the lake. Wow, no mucking about with her, she's right into it.

'I am Tobias Kent, the person who spoke to Detective Carland originally. The body is actually in my cabin, over there,' Tobias says a bit sheepishly, stepping toward them and pointing to his cabin.

'I thought the victim was killed in a houseboat fire?' Sutton asks, looking puzzled. A small wrinkle forms between her eyebrows.

'Yes, but we could not just leave him in the pouring rain.'

She holds her hand up in a *stop right there* gesture. 'Don't tell me you *moved* the body?'

'Yes.'

Her mouth is hard set and she can barely contain her anger. 'That means you've contaminated the original crime scene, effectively creating a second crime scene. You have compromised the integrity of any evidence we find.' She glances at Constable Couttas, who looks equally annoyed.

Finaly, some legit police procedure. I'm taking mental notes of everything they say and do. I knew that Tobias was contaminating the crime scene by moving the body, so I feel quite smug that it's brought up by them as a concern now. I hope it doesn't affect the chances of catching the killer.

'We could not leave him on the jetty in the middle of a storm in the middle of the night. It would have been inhumane,' explains Tobias.

'A crime scene *must* be preserved.' Her arms are folded across her chest now.

'It was a torrential storm. Whatever evidence you might be looking for would surely have been washed away.'

'Not necessarily,' Sutton takes a deep breath. 'Anyway, what's done is done. Constable Couttas, can you go and secure what's left of the primary crime scene, while I look at the secondary scene, please?'

He gives her a confused look.

'The houseboat. Go and secure the boat while I look at this body they moved.'

Couttas nods once. He walks back to their vehicle and pulls out a large roll of police tape from the boot before turning and heading down toward the lake. He walks like a cowboy, legs wide, deliberate steps. It might just be him trying not to slip over in the mud, but either way it looks funny.

Tobias starts to walk back toward his cabin. Shell and I follow him. Sutton raises an eyebrow at us.

'We were there when he was found,' Shell says by way of explanation.

And we don't want to miss a thing.

Tobias opens his front door and leads Sutton through to the spare room.

'I should warn you, there is an odour now,' he says. Sutton takes a face mask out of her pocket and pulls on some blue rubber gloves. Tobias slowly opens the door and she steps in, closing the door behind her. Even for the seconds that the door is open, the smell overwhelming. I feel it tear up my nose and almost into my mouth. Shell looks like she's feeling the same. It's a lot. Like burnt meat that has gone off.

We don't follow. While I want to hear everything, I don't want to see him again. Once was enough.

Shell and I stand with our ears against the closed door to listen in.

Tobias's voice comes first, muffled slightly. 'We found him dead on the jetty. We believe he tried to get out of the houseboat but his foot got stuck in the fence wire on the jetty and he died from his burns.'

Sutton clears her throat. 'What alerted you to the fire in the first place?'

'Someone saw the fire on the lake from the front cabin. I should mention now that I thought I heard an explosion earlier in the evening but decided it was probably thunder. Now I realise it may have been the boat.'

'Okay. You found the body, and then you carried him up here?'

'Yes.'

'And no one's touched him since?' The floorboards creak as someone moves around.

'No. I came in to open a window once the storm was over this morning as the odour was getting overwhelming.'

What about the watch?

Sutton makes an annoyed sound before continuing. 'Were you alone when you discovered the body?'

'No, Cath, who you met earlier, was there, as well as Gus and Shell, the kids outside, and their friend Kane, who is around here somewhere.'

'And what time was this?'

'Shell saw the fire around 6.45 pm. We went down to the jetty right away and found him there. He was burnt extensively. He must have been right in the middle of the blast.'

We can hear what sounds like a sheet being pulled back. There's an intake of breath.

'Brutal,' she says softly. 'This explosion you mentioned hearing earlier. Tell me about it.'

'It was a loud boom, but the storm was so noisy that I didn't pay that much attention. Initially I put it down to thunder or a tree falling down.'

'Perhaps the engine was faulty?' she suggests.

'I think the boat was tampered with, and the explosion was deliberate.'

'Well. That's a big allegation,' Sutton sounds surprised. 'What evidence do you have?'

'I found this at the scene.'

There's a rustling noise, presumably as Tobias pulls the gizmo out to show Sutton.

'You took this from the crime scene *as well*? Potential evidence?' She somehow manages to sound even more annoyed.

'Yes,' he replies. 'It looked important. I took it in case the houseboat sank before you people arrived here.' *That's a good answer*, I think to myself.

Her voice sounds beyond exasperated. 'Forensics will need to see this.'

There's a moment of silence before Sutton speaks again. 'What's that round section in the middle, do you think?'

'I do not know. It looks familiar, but I cannot place it.'

'Hmm. Now then, if this was deliberate, who do you think did it? And why?'

'I really do not know.'

Shell and I look at each other. We both must look strange, our mouths covered with the top collar of our jumpers to ward off the worst of the stench.

'I like the ways she asks all these blunt questions,' whispers Shell. 'No nonsense.'

'Do you—'

The door suddenly opens and we both spring back in shock.

'Listening at doors now?' Tobias tuts, while Sutton removes her mask.

'No! We were just . . .' I've got nothing.

Sutton takes off her gloves and shoves them in her pocket.

'What's the procedure now?' I ask eagerly.

Sutton takes us through the process. 'As the local police first on the scene, we're here to secure the scene and get some statements to form a basic picture of what's happened. Once we've done our preliminary work, a detective from the Criminal Investigation Unit will come and investigate fully. Given our remote location, we will also likely have a homicide team and an arson team come up from Melbourne to forensically examine the crime.'

'Why both?' Shell asks.

'Homicide will look at the body for cause of death, while the arson team will look at what caused the fire,' I reply, before Sutton can respond.

Sutton looks impressed.

'I read up on this kind of stuff. I want to join the police one day,' I explain goofily.

'I wanted to join from about your age too,' she says, giving me a half smile. Suddenly she seems more human. She grabs her chunky satellite phone and calls her colleague. 'Couttas, we're coming down to the houseboat.'

'Copy,' comes the crackled reply.

As we walk out the door, Sutton turns to Tobias. 'I want you to lock all the doors and windows. We need to keep this site secure until a detective can have a look and make an informed assessment of what has happened here. Does anyone else have a key?'

'Cath will have one. She's in cabin one.'

'Right, we'll pick that up on the way through.'

Together we walk over to Cath's cabin. I like the confident way Sutton strides, despite the mud. She exudes control and authority.

Shell and I hold back while there is a discussion at Cath's front door. Nash emerges from the cabin with a key. Sutton then walks over to the police car, opens up the door, and pulls out another roll of police tape. She strides back to Tobias's cabin and prepares to tape up the door.

'How am I meant to get in and out?'

'You aren't. You'll need to stay somewhere else for now. You can't be here until the team has cleared the scene.'

He sighs, resigned to the fact that there appears to be no arguing with her. 'I'll stay in one of the other cabins then. Can I collect a couple of my things first? Under your supervision, of course.'

She nods and follows him back inside. A couple of minutes later they re-emerge, Tobias carrying a small bag, his laptop and his notebook.

Sutton finishes taping up Tobias's door and then heads down the hill to the jetty. We follow along behind them, desperate not to miss a thing. Sutton either doesn't care, or doesn't notice us. Down the hill, Constable Couttas is standing near the jetty with his arms folded, like a bouncer outside a nightclub.

Silently, Couttas and Sutton put on rubber gloves and carefully step onto the houseboat. They look around, examining each section methodically. I can see them at the back of the houseboat, looking at the remains of the engine.

Watching them search the wreckage, I keep thinking about what it must have been like for Walker. How scared was he? How much pain was he in? I like to think that the fire burnt his nerve endings or whatever, but that might just be a myth I've read.

Sutton points to the engine's surrounds. 'He found the device here. He thinks the engine was deliberately fixed to explode. Obviously the detective and the arson investigators will look into this, so we just need to preserve the scene, especially here.'

Couttas nods. 'Affirmative.'

After a few minutes, Sutton steps back up onto the jetty and walks toward us. She's holding an oddly shaped piece of metal, a bit bigger than a fifty-cent coin. 'Bag,' she calls to Couttas. He takes a plastic evidence bag and pen out of his jacket pocket and passes them to her. She puts the item in and writes something on the label before sealing it.

'What's that?' I ask.

'I'm not sure yet,' Sutton replies.

It's wrong how much I am enjoying this. It's like a cop show coming to life before my eyes. I want to watch and learn everything.

Once they are finished on the houseboat, Couttas starts to use police tape to cover up the entrance to the houseboat and the fence railing where it was tied to the jetty. It makes a satisfying noise as it is pulled from the large roll and stretched out.

Now it's a proper crime scene.

Chapter 30

Notebook

Later Sutton gets us all together in Cath's cabin. Everything seems to happen here now. Parties, meals, revelations, fights, and now police interviews.

Everyone is looking tired and frazzled. With tempers running high and accusations flying about, they are not the united crew they seemed to be when we first got here.

Sutton asks Tobias to repeat what he told her and bring out the gizmo he found again. Then she opens up her official police notebook, looks around the rest of us and clears her throat. 'Did anyone else hear this boom that Tobias alleges he heard?'

Everybody shakes their head.

'How do you blow up a houseboat? Do you pour petrol around the engine and wait for someone to start it up, or do you just drop a match and run off?' Kane asks enthusiastically.

Sutton smiles, just a little. 'Pouring petrol around the engine would be easier. Light that and you'd have time to run off.'

'How long?'

'It completely depends. Five minutes, perhaps. In this weather, maybe a bit longer, given the engine is at the back of the vessel and semi-exposed to the rain.'

Kane nods like he is some kind of expert now. 'So you're saying that someone would have time to run back, hide the petrol, and be back here by the time the engine exploded?'

'In theory, yes. But let's remember the device Tobias retrieved from the houseboat. Ignoring the fact that he has been removing evidence from a crime scene – *for now* – it does look like an incendiary device. This indeed points to the fire being deliberately lit, but let's see what the detective and homicide and arson have to say. My job is to just secure the scene and talk to you all to get a basic sense of what has happened here.'

'But don't we only have one person's word that there was a deliberate explosion at all? Could that gadget just have been planted there to throw you off?' Shell asks innocently.

Sutton eyes Shell with curiosity. 'Well, yes, it could have happened another way. But that's why we have arson investigators coming.'

Tobias gives Shell a strange look. 'You don't believe me?'

'Just exploring options. *You* are the only one who heard the explosion. *You* are the one telling us the time of the fire. *You* are the one who supposedly found the gizmo that caused the fire. *You* are the one who moved the body. *You* are the one who claims the watch is missing. I'm just saying that everything about this case revolves around your word.'

He frowns at her. 'Why would I lie?'

Shell shrugs innocently.

'What's this about a watch?' Sutton asks.

Shell's smiles faintly as Tobias's face falls. He turns to Sutton. 'Walker wore a valuable watch. He was wearing it when we found his body, but it has gone . . . missing . . . since he has been in my cabin.'

Sutton is frowning. 'These two things may be linked or may be entirely separate. Either way, this shouldn't be the first I'm hearing of it.' She looks like she's thinking for a moment, then turns to the rest of us. 'Did one of you take this watch?'

Everyone says no or shakes their head. Shell's laser eyes scan everyone's reactions.

'Can you tell me what this watch looks like?' Sutton looks to Tobias.

Tobias shows her the website on his phone. 'I think you should search everyone's cabin for the watch, before they have a chance to leave the community.'

'That's a very overpriced timepiece,' she says, her eyebrows high with surprise. 'But our job is not to look for missing watches, whether connected to the crime or not. Our job, as I keep repeating, is to secure the crime scenes and take preliminary statements from each of you. Now, is this everyone who was present on Saturday night?'

'Yes. This is all of us,' says Cath.

'And you all knew the victim?'

Everyone nods.

'Except for us. We only met him briefly when we arrived on Saturday,' I say, pointing to Shell and Kane and me.

'Right,' Sutton looks back to Cath. 'Tobias tells me that you all had an altercation with Mr Walker on Saturday, between 3.30 pm and 3.45 pm – is that correct?'

Cath clears her throat. 'It wasn't an altercation. It was just a disagreement. It didn't last long and it didn't really mean anything.'

That's an interesting interpretation of events.

Sutton frowns at her. 'Alright then. Did any of you have reason to believe he was on that houseboat?'

'We all saw him drive away, back toward the main road,' says Maxine. Around her, everyone murmurs in agreement. 'Then the storm really hit, and nobody wanted to be outside. None of us knew that he'd come back, or gone to the houseboat.'

'And you were all here together? No one was unaccounted for at any time?'

Cath gets in before anyone else can answer. 'We were all here together the whole time, until we saw the fire.'

Sutton suddenly gets a call on her phone. I can hear a crackly voice but not what is being said. 'Right sir, affirmative.'

Sutton puts her hand over the receiver and addresses the room. 'Detective Carland from the criminal investigation unit will be here in two hours.' She turns to Couttas. 'Constable, can you get everyone's full name and address for me? Once you're done, return to the houseboat. I'll guard the cabin with the victim.'

Couttas nods. 'On it.'

Sutton continues talking on her phone as she marches off to Tobias's cabin. Meanwhile, Couttas takes out his notepad and starts taking people's details. Once he's finished, he leaves to the houseboat. There's a sense of anticlimax in the air. Even though the police are here, we're still waiting for a detective to take over the investigation properly.

Tobias turns to Shell and me. 'I still think we need to find that watch. We should tell everyone that we're going to look around their cabins, get their consent.'

Shell and I look at each other excitedly. Maybe our investigation isn't quite over after all.

Chapter 31

Petrol

Tobias explains to everyone that he wants to search all the cabins for the watch. 'With you present to observe, of course.'

'You already looked in our cabins before,' whines Greta.

'If the police aren't bothered about the watch, why are you?' adds Maxine, awkwardly adjusting her bra strap under her top. Is she wearing more make-up than before?

'Got something to hide?' Nash snickers.

Greta mumbles something and Maxine shakes her head.

'I can come along and be an independent witness?' I say.

'Just to snoop, more like,' Maxine scoffs.

Tobias turns to her. 'Gus can make sure I do not steal anything or plant the watch there myself.' It's like he read my mind.

'What if Gus is the one who took it? Or maybe you did, Professor,' snarks Nash. It's not an entirely unreasonable thing to say, but it annoys me.

Tobias turns to him. 'I will be going through the kids' cabin too.'

Smiling at Shell, I follow Tobias and Greta over to her cabin. She plods along in the mud, clearly not happy about this.

Tobias has a quick look around and asks Greta to open this cupboard and that drawer, while she lifts things and moves things around for him.

While looking into her colourful wardrobe, Tobias points to a blanket, which is covering something at the back. 'What's under there?'

'Dunno,' she says, her eyes darting around.

'Would you move the blanket for me, please?'

Greta reluctantly lifts it up.

'No!' she yells as the blanket reveals a metal jerry can there, marked 'Marine Petrol'.

Greta starts to cry, shouting at the same time. 'Not mine! It's *not* mine. It wasn't there yesterday,' she sobs.

'Then where did it come from?' Tobias asks.

Cath appears at the door, with the others all following behind. They must have heard her shouting.

She looks at the jerry can in Tobias's hand and the look on Greta's face. Cath shakes her head in stunned disbelief. 'You did this?'

Greta gulps in a breath and then swipes a decent amount of snot from her nose. 'That's not mine.'

'You took a man's life!' Cath has teared up now and the look of disappointment on her face is palpable. Greta looks horrified.

Suddenly she spots Nash, smirking in the background. 'You put this here!' she yells, pointing at him.

He just grins, rubbing his hands together, not bothering to hide his pleasure.

Cath glares at Nash. 'Did you?'

'No,' he says, the smile wiped off of his face. 'She's lying.' But I can't help feeling like he's the one who's lying.

'How did she do it if she was with me? We were sitting in Cath's lounge from 5.30 to 6, setting out food,' Shell protests.

Nash shrugs. 'She must have done it earlier.'

'Any earlier and it would have been light, so we would have seen the flames.'

'I don't know *how* she managed it, but I am sure that she did it,' Nash responds.

It's hard to argue with his logic. But I'm also distracted. These people are liars. They know something about Jane and I can't stop thinking about it. I have no pity for any of them right now.

'Does the generator or anything else here require petrol like this?' Shell asks. She looks upset, but she's no match for Cath, who looks devastated.

'No.'

Tobias sighs. 'Having a jerry can of petrol doesn't mean Greta is responsible, but it is suspicious. I will have to tell Sutton.'

Greta makes a moaning noise and runs into her bedroom. Maxine moves to follow her.

'Leave her,' says Cath, her voice shaking. 'It's not like she can go anywhere.'

Tobias stops and touches her arm gently. 'I know this is damning, but this does not absolutely mean she did it.'

'Doesn't it?' Cath sighs, pulling at her jumper that now boasts a hole where she's pulled out another thread.

Chapter 32

Account

Tobias gestures to us. 'We should keep going before Sutton realises what we are doing and steps in.'

We leave as Sutton arrives. Over my shoulder I can see Cath meeting Sutton on the verandah and gesturing toward the jerry can. Nash is wearing that same smug grin as before, still clearly enjoying it all. I turn back around and focus on the job at hand.

'Why are you so invested in this?' Shell asks Tobias as we walk. 'You acted like we were ridiculous before, but suddenly you're taking us seriously.'

'Yes. I am sorry about that. It is bothering me that someone desecrated a dead body to steal a ridiculous watch.'

As we approach Tobias's cabin, Kane takes out his phone and takes a selfie with the police tape around Tobias's door in the background.

'Hey, that's not cool. This is serious! You aren't posting these, are you?' I groan.

He looks sheepishly at me. I pull up his Insta profile, scrolling through his latest posts. As I flick past selfies he's shared, a second account gets suggested to me, with a headless torso that looks very familiar. Is that . . . Kane's sixpack?

'Hang on, you have a second account?' I say, surprised.

'Yeah, it's something I keep separate actually.'

It's a bunch of snaps of him with his head cropped out. These are way more revealing than his usual pics, more posed. I roll my eyes. Then I notice the name of this account. 'Kane's Gainz?' I burst out laughing.

Shell honks out a laugh too.

'What?' he snaps, quite defensive.

I can't stop laughing long enough to explain, so he keeps talking. 'There's nothing wrong with showing off my hard work. Girls love it. Guys do too for that matter. I don't have a job so this is a legit way of trying to get some cash.' He looks so crestfallen as he speaks that we both stop laughing.

'I'm not laughing at the pics,' I say. 'Just your username. It's kinda cringe.'

He looks relieved, but also annoyed at the same time. 'It's meant to be funny.'

He crosses his arms and goes quiet. For once this isn't a move to show off his guns but an actual response.

'I'm sorry. If it's meant to take the piss then that's cool.'

I forget that even with his increasingly big muscles, he's as vulnerable and self-conscious as the rest of us sometimes. Who knows what really drives his weights obsession? I just thought it was an extension of his love of footy, but now that I've seen him sleepwalking and taking steroids, it's clearly something more. I really have to talk to him properly. Soon, but not now.

'Don't joke about it. I don't have a go at you for eating junk food all the time and not doing any exercise, do I?' he says pointedly.

Ouch. 'Well, I think you just did . . . but no.'

He's right, he never does. Certainly not as often as I mock his muscle bro exploits and huge ego.

'Sorry, I forget your guns don't make you bulletproof,' I smile.

'All good,' he says flatly.

'And the pictures do look good. I mean, if you're into that kinda thing.'

'Right, like you're not. Gay guys love muscles.'

'Not all of us,' I say, though I'm pretty sure he's actually right. Thing is, as he gets bigger and bigger, it's getting harder to distinguish him – my mate – from all the other muscle bros out there. He's starting to look like one of them.

I unconsciously pull down my shirt to make sure my love handles are covered. The thought of posing without a shirt in any situation, online or otherwise, fills me with horror. I would literally die.

Up ahead, Maxine unlocks the door of her cabin and walks in, followed by Tobias.

I look back at my phone to avoid his eyes. 'You posted that annoying selfie from the day we got here? The one you took when we were trying to get in to our cabin?' I say.

'Yeah, once we got reception back. You haven't already seen it and liked it?' Kane grins.

I pinch the screen to zoom in on the pic. Beyond Kane's bicep is a shadow in the distance. It's the shape of someone heading to the lake.

'What time did you take this?' I say, pointing to the background. 'There's someone down by the lake.'

'I'll check the original,' says Kane, scrolling. 'Okay yeah, it was taken at 5.40. But that's too early, right?'

'Yeah,' I say, disappointed. It's too early. If it had been like thirty or forty minutes later, then it would have helped. That would have been the clue of the century if somehow Kane had captured the killer disappearing into the distance beyond his guns.

'Who is it?' asks Shell, taking the phone and zooming in. She even squints with one eye closed.

'It could be literally anyone,' I say. 'Everyone here has those big black jackets that Cath bought, even us. You can't tell one person from another in the rain.'

'Actually,' says Kane. 'I think I know who it is.'

He uses his fingers to zoom in on the figure as much as possible. There's a hint of leopard skin fabric coming out the sleeve of the jacket.

Maxine.

Chapter 33

Soil

'What was she going to the houseboat for?' asks Shell, pinching the bridge of her nose.

'Maybe she was hooking up with him too,' says Kane slowly. 'She's flirty with almost anyone.'

I wonder about Maxine. In some ways she's the last person I could imagine being capable of murder. She seems too sloppy to have planned anything like this.

'Come on, let's help Tobias,' I say, walking up the steps of Maxine's verandah. Kane knocks on the door.

Maxine appears, holding her arms open to wave us inside. Tobias has been waiting for us to start the search. He begins with the cupboards in the kitchen and then the lounge. Maxine looks on, smiling, incongruously eating ice cream straight from the tub. It's like she's observing a TV show happen around her.

'Why would I want this watch?' she asks between mouthfuls.

'It's worth a lot of money,' I say.

'So what? I have all I need here. A roof over my head, friends, peace and quiet. Until recently that is . . .'

Tobias searches the bedroom with Shell watching from the doorway. He comes out shaking his head. Shell has a puzzled expression on her face.

Once the search is over, Maxine looks relieved.

'Hang on,' I say. 'Let's go back outside.'

Everyone looks confused, but they follow as I head out the front door and walk over the other side of the cabins to the veggie patch. I'm searching for whatever Greta said Maxine was burying. And then I find it.

'There!' I point to a section of the garden that looks like it's freshly dug up. 'Remember Greta said she saw her digging in the middle of the storm?'

The soil is still muddy from the rain, but this section of dirt looks newer compared to the others. No weeds, not even tiny ones. Maxine looks pale. I grab the pitchfork that's leaning against the side of the house and start to dig.

'Stop!' she shouts.

I see the panic on her face, but I keep going. Putting the watch in a box and burying it would be a great way to hide it until you had a chance to sell it somehow. Suddenly the pitchfork hits something solid and there's a cracking sound. *Oh shit, have I broken the watch?*

'Stop, don't touch it!' she shouts again as I reach into the dirt.

'Why, afraid I'll find the watch?'

'No,' she says, as she walks over and grabs the pitchfork off me. 'Afraid you'll cut yourself.'

She uses the pitchfork to gently move some soil aside revealing a pile of empty wine and spirit bottles, including one that's smashed.

'What is all this about?' asks Tobias.

I feel so bad for her. Trying to speak softly, I ask, 'Are you afraid of people realising how much you drink? My mum used to hide hers under boxes in the recycling.'

Her face crumples. 'I thought it might be better here, if I started a new life, but ...' she rubs her eyes. 'It never let's go. It's cost me everything and I still can't stop. Happy now?' she stomps back into her cabin and slams the door.

We all look at each other guiltily.

Tobias half-smiles at me. 'It is not your fault. It was a good idea to see what she was hiding.'

'Maybe, but we're still no closer to finding the watch.'

Shell clears her throat. 'I did see something when I was looking into her bedroom. That plastic thing she hangs her earrings on. There's a silver gum leaf earring missing. I wonder if it's the metal thing Sutton found on the houseboat?'

She cracks her fingers, grinning. Damn she's good.

Tobias shrugs. 'Could be. Cath's cabin is next.'

I look toward cabin four, where John lives. 'What about there?'

'No,' says Tobias, 'He is not here to give permission. I've already gone in once. No one else has been in there.'

I'm desperate to get into that cabin now.

It's like Shell can read my mind. 'Cath keeps all the keys on that hook in the kitchen,' she whispers.

Chapter 34

Envelope

At Cath's cabin, it feels weird to be looking around her stuff, given the level of (begrudging) hospitality she's shown us. She is underwhelmed by this search. Her eyes look tired, with dark bags under them.

'I can promise that you will not find that ridiculous watch here,' she says to Tobias. She's sitting at the kitchen table working on her laptop, but she keeps looking up, staring out the window.

I see Shell eyeing off the keys on the hook by the kitchen cupboards.

'Has anyone told Walker's father yet?' Cath asks out of the blue, addressing no one in particular. It's a good question.

'His son is dead and he may not know. Meanwhile, here I am doing paperwork.'

Tobias puts his hand on her shoulder. 'There is nothing wrong with distracting yourself from something upsetting. Senior Constable Sutton said that nothing can happen until the detective gets here, so I presume we cannot say anything to anyone until that has happened.'

'How long before the detective gets here? I feel awful with him just stuck in your spare room, alone.' Cath wipes a tear from her eye.

'Not much longer, I'd say,' Tobias pats her on the arm before moving to the middle of the room to start the search.

As he starts moving books on the bookcase, Cath jerks her head up. 'Don't get them out of order please, I like them just the way they are.' I didn't realise she was so fastidious. Or is it a ruse to stop him from finding the watch?

Nash of course is just standing by the door, scowling at us as usual.

'Shall we look at your room next, Nash?' says Tobias.

Shell points through the window. Sutton is heading our way.

'Gus, can you look in Nash's room while I look in Cath's please?'

'Yes,' I say a little too quickly.

A hint of a smirk crosses Kane's face. 'I'll do the bathroom.'

'Why would I take his bullshit watch?' Nash says as we go into his room.

'Because it's worth heaps,' I say. I'm actually nervous about going into his room. It feels quite intimate.

Opening the door, I am totally unsurprised to see that it's a mess. The bed covers are bundled in a heap. There are piles of clothes on the floor, and car magazines spread everywhere else. You can barely see the carpet. His Nintendo and phone charger and the leather bands he wears on his wrists are lying on the bedside table. Various metal band posters are on the walls, and he has a blackout curtain over the window.

He sits on his bed, leaning back on a pillow that he's propped up between himself and the wall. He watches me as I open the wardrobe and start to look through his stuff, checking pockets in jackets and jeans.

'You're getting warmer.'

I ignore him. I'm too distracted by the fact that his clothes smell like him and I don't hate it. I feel like by touching his clothes like this, I'm kind of touching him.

The next drawer I open is full of his undies, so I get him to show me there's nothing there himself. Touching them myself would be too weird.

I get down on my knees and look under the bed. There's a few shoeboxes with nothing of interest inside them, and nothing else.

'You done now?' he says, standing up and moving to the door.

'No.'

There's something about the way he was sitting on the bed the whole time that makes me suspicious. The pillow he was leaning on looks normal, slightly bent in the middle with a crinkled cover. But the other cover looks flat and rigid.

I reach for it.

'What are you doing?'

'Having a look here. Getting warmer now, am I?'

'Don't.'

But it's too late. I yank the pillow off the bed and stick my hand in the pillowcase, pulling out a big yellow envelope. It's addressed to Simon Walker.

'What's this?' I ask, waving the envelope at him.

'Give it here!' He looks panicked.

I realise that it's not sealed. When I go to pull out what's inside, he tries to rip it from my hand. My grip is stronger.

I scan the first bit of the front page, my mouth open. I turn and dash into the lounge, brandishing the letter, with Nash trying to claw it out of my hands.

'I thought you said you were determined not to sell?'

Cath frowns. 'I am.'

'Then why is there a sale contract here for this land, signed and ready to go?' I say dramatically.

Chapter 35

Contract

'Give me that!' Cath snaps at me. But Tobias reaches out and deftly takes the papers from my hand before Cath can get to them. She yelps with frustration, colour rising up her neck to her cheeks.

He skims the pages quickly. 'Hold on. There are two copies here, both dated three days ago. Why were you talking to Walker as if it was never going to happen, when all the time you were ready to sell?'

She looks guiltily over at Nash. 'It's complicated.' His eyes are cast down toward his feet.

'It seems very simple to me,' Tobias replies. 'You were willing to sell the land to him and, according to this, grant him full access *and* ownership of the circle too! Oh Cath, why?'

'There's more at stake in the world than your bloody stone circle!' she barks, snatching the papers back. 'Stop living in the past and come to terms with the present.'

'The past informs the present. The circle is significant.'

'You're so one-eyed that you forget about what's happening around you—'

She stops when she realises what she's said. Tobias instinctively puts his hand to his eye patch.

'Sorry, I didn't mean . . .' she steels herself before continuing. 'It's my land and I will do what I want with it.'

I don't get it. 'If you were ready to sell it to him and had signed the contracts, then why are the papers hidden here?'

Cath puts her head in her hands. 'I panicked. I took both copies back and ran out of his office.'

'You changed your mind?' I ask.

'I had a wave of doubt and said I needed the three-day cooling-off period to think.'

'Think about what exactly? It sounds like you had made up your mind,' says Tobias, anger in his voice. 'Oh wait, you had to think about telling us. Especially Greta and Maxine. I am furious, but the community will be devastated. This is their home.'

Shell's one step ahead, as usual. 'This is the secret Walker threatened to reveal, isn't it? Not that you were an item, but that you'd agreed to sell.'

Cath doesn't seem to register Shell. 'You can't tell them Tobias, not yet. Promise me.'

'Can I ask a stupid question?' asks Kane.

'Better than anyone I know,' laughs Shell.

'Now that he's dead, is the contract still valid?'

Cath shrugs slightly. 'It's complex. Technically the contract is still valid if his estate wishes to complete the transaction. But there is also an exit clause. I am waiting to hear back from my lawyer about this.'

'So not only have you sold the land, but you have probably now handed it to Batholomew Walker, who is even more ruthless than his son, and who has the money and resources to fight any kind of historical protection I try to get on the circle and just gut this place . . .' Tobias's voice gets higher and higher the angrier he gets.

Cath looks panicked. 'I think my lawyer can rescind this contract but I'm not completely sure yet.'

Tobias shakes his head in frustration.

Cath turns back to us, hands clasped together. 'Please, you kids *can't* tell Greta and Maxine. Let me get an answer from my lawyer first. No need to panic them if I can rescind. Right?'

She glares at us and we nod our agreement. Even with the chips down, she's still a strong force.

Shell looks like she's about to say something else when Sutton turns up at the front door.

Sutton takes in the scene but doesn't seem to notice anything odd about the way we're looking at each other. She directs her gaze at Cath. 'I want to ask you some questions about your tenants here, please.'

Cath nods and sits back on the couch, pushing the contract envelope aside.

I want to stay and hear what she has to say, but we use this distraction to get out of here. As the three of us leave, I whisper to Shell and Kane. 'Cath is tough, even when cornered. I wouldn't want to cross her.'

'A hundred per cent,' says Kane.

'Thing is, is she ruthless enough to light that fire?'

'Why would she, if she had agreed to sell anyway?'

'She changed her mind. What if he wouldn't let her take it back?' I suggest unconvincingly. It doesn't sound plausible enough.

Shell meanwhile is waving her hand around in circles. A keyring hangs off her finger.

'Is that the key to the mysterious cabin four?' I gasp.

She just grins. Respect. Even Kane looks at her in admiration.

'We can't go now though, someone might see us,' she says quietly. 'We should go back to our cabin for a bit and wait for the right time.'

Kane nods and starts to follow Shell back to cabin six. In the corner of my eye, I notice Nash sitting outside his cabin, throwing rocks at the sign again. He sees me and frowns.

'Why did you have it hidden in your room? Why didn't she hide it herself?'

Nash stands up and swirls the mud around with his feet. 'I thought he might come looking for it. I knew he'd never come into my room, too grubby for his fancy arse.'

He juts his chin over toward Greta, who is sitting on a seat at the front of her cabin, fiddling with some piece of equipment.

'She thinks she's fooling us, saying she's great with fixing the generator and stuff, but it's all a lie. She couldn't even fix the professor's toaster or Maxine's clock. She just wants to make herself look important.' There's real venom in his voice.

'Wow, you really hate her, don't you? Is that why you put the petrol in her cabin?'

'Duh. She wants me gone. I have to stop her.'

Just how far would you go to stop her?

Chapter 36

Wall

Later, Kane and I are playing ping pong in the garage. Unsurprisingly, Kane is much better than me. His serves are brutal. Mine are hopeless.

'I think I know why you're sleepwalking,' I say, serving the ping pong ball awkwardly toward him.

'Okay, why?' he asks, swatting the ball back easily.

'Steroids. I looked up the ones you're using. They have heaps of side effects, including three or four things related to sleep.' I weakly hit it back to his side of the net.

He smashes the ball back at me and I miss it completely. 'How did you find out?'

'I looked in your bag for . . . um . . . toothpaste, and saw the bottle and needles.' I pick up the ball from where it's landed behind me, grateful that he can't see my face.

'What the hell!' he snaps. 'It's not cool for you to just go through my bag!'

That's rich, coming from you, I think to myself.

'I'm sorry, I'm just worried about you.' I serve badly.

He hits it back hard and I miss again.

Suddenly he drops his paddle and puts his head in his hands. 'I didn't want anyone to know.'

'When did you start?'

He looks up and runs his hand through his hair. 'After my knee reconstruction last year, I got really out of shape. I just wanted some help to get back on track. And one of the guys at gym seemed to be getting bigger every day, so I asked him for advice. He told me he used this stuff, and one thing led to another.'

'No wonder you're so aggro lately. You've got fake hormones running through your body.'

'That's not what they are, but yeah, I do feel weird sometimes.'

'You have to stop. Your parents are right. What if you did sleepwalk out onto the road or off a bridge or something even worse? Your gains aren't worth dying for.'

'I know, I know. But it's hard too, because I like how big I'm getting, and all the attention.'

'Think of all the attention you'll get at your funeral,' I snap.

Shell walks into the garage. The two of us aren't looking at each other.

'What have I missed?' she asks. 'Gossip?'

'Nothing,' we say at the same time.

She doesn't believe us, I can tell.

'Okay then, keep your secrets.' Kane and I avoid her eyes. 'I came up here because I feel like we're running out of time to solve this. The detective could be here any minute now.'

I nod. 'Okay, let's see what we've got.'

She holds up one finger. 'Greta has gone up the list now we know she had the petrol, which looks really suspicious. She has a big motive. But she still has an alibi – she was with me.'

'I think Nash put the petrol in her cabin. They hate each other,' I say.

Kane raises his eyebrows. 'She's still my pick. She's nuts, so anything is possible. Could she have known about the contract? Would that have sent her over the edge?'

I shrug. 'She would be the last person Cath would tell, because she'd know how upset she'd be.'

Shell holds up a second finger. 'Maxine. Still has the same motive. Still has the opportunity. The burying of the bottles doesn't really change anything.'

'I think she's our strongest suspect,' I say. 'She went down to the houseboat that day before the party, but we don't know why yet.'

A third finger goes up. 'Cath is my pick. She was going to sell but changed her mind. Where does that leave her now? I think she'd be ruthless when it comes to protecting Nash, if Walker had threatened him.'

I shake my head. 'Cath already had both of the contracts, and she said herself that the place is still hers even though she's signed the papers.'

Kane looks at me. 'What about Nash?'

Shell holds up a fourth finger. 'He wants to leave The Circle. He wanted her to sell to Walker. Killing him makes no sense.'

She holds out her thumb. 'Which brings us to Tobias.'

'What exactly is his motive? I mean, sure, Walker went at him, but he gave as good as he got,' I say. 'He came here at Cath's request to look into the stones. He's not hiding from the world like the others.'

'Or is he, but just in a different way?' asks Shell, looking right at me.

'The professor is obsessed with the stone circle. I bet he'd do anything to protect it . . . but would he kill for it?' Kane says.

'Walker did hint that he knew some secret of Tobias's too,' I say.

'Don't forget, it's all guesswork really. The timing of when the fire started is based on Tobias's word, no actual evidence,' Shell reminds me.

I nod. 'That's true.'

'So we've hit a wall with that side of things. On that note,' Shell waves the key to cabin four in the air again. 'We better do this now, before the detective arrives.'

'You're right. We need to piece this together now.'

They're all connected, I know it. To each other. And to Jane, somehow. I just can't seem to unravel all of this. The knots are too big for me to pull it all apart and find out how it fits together. I can't shake the feeling that this John is linked to Jane. The whole community seems to be lying about something and why should John be any different? I have to find out what's happening in that cabin.

Kane suddenly looks determined. 'Let's go. I'll distract Sutton while you two go in there and see what you can find.'

Shell looks concerned. 'I'm afraid to ask this, but . . . how exactly will you distract her?'

'Gun show,' he laughs.

Shell and I look at each other in horror.

'I'm joking!' he laughs. 'Women find me hot, all ages. I won't have to show her the guns.'

I peek out of the garage roller door. I can't quite see Tobias's front door from this angle, so I can't tell whether Sutton is still standing guard. Slowly I edge my way along the wall of the shed and look again. She's still there, talking on a satellite phone. I can't quite hear what she's saying, but I imagine she's speaking to the investigative team or her station. I duck back into the shed.

'Now!'

Kane rolls his shirt sleeves up and moves toward Sutton. Shell and I hold back, waiting to see what he does. He needs to move her away from the door a bit so we're not in her eyeline as we go into the other cabin. As he approaches, Sutton hangs up her phone. Kane smiles and says something to her. He points toward the houseboat. She looks over but doesn't move. He waves more enthusiastically and she seems to resign herself to looking. As she moves further out from the house, Shell and I run around the other side and to the front door of cabin four.

Shell slips the key into the lock, pushes her bulk against the door, and opens it just enough for both of us to sneak in.

It's quite dark inside, despite the light outside, because the blinds are drawn. I flick on a light switch and the main room comes to life.

This place is definitely an artist's cabin. There are dozens of paintings on stretched canvases, all of them full of dark and moody colours and strange images. They're hanging on what looks like every available piece of wall. They are unnerving, especially en masse. *What kind of person paints such sinister images?*

There's a big table in one corner that's covered in tubes of paint, brushes and turps. There's a few mixing containers and an easel standing next to the table, by the window. I lift the blind and see this cabin has a clear view of the stone circle, like ours. I open the window a bit as it's so stuffy in here.

Shell rustles through the kitchen. 'What are we even looking for?' she asks, opening and closing cupboards.

I keep looking around the living area. 'Something that links him to Jane. Or something that links him to Walker or the fire. I dunno, really, I know it's a stretch.'

We search in silence for a bit, opening cupboards and pulling out drawers.

'Hey, so, I get the feeling that you really like Greta.'

Shell stares into space, as if deciding something. 'Do you know what ace is?'

'Ace as in the companion from *Doctor Who*?'

She rolls her eyes. 'Ugh. No. Ace as in asexual.'

'Oh. Yeah, I do.' *Gulp.*

'I think I'm ace. That's why all Kane's macho sexualised talk is making me angry. Apart from it being so basic, I just don't feel that way – about anyone. I never have.'

I try to find the right words. 'Never? Maybe you just haven't . . . met the right person. How long have you felt like this?'

Tears form in her eyes. I know immediately that this was the wrong thing to say. Shell never cries, never loses it. 'I've met lots of people that I could vibe with, in theory, but I just feel nothing. Like I feel great friendship or admiration and stuff, but no sexual feelings. At all.'

'What does your psych say?'

'They say that it's fine, it's just a way of being, like anything else. To not worry about it or try to force something that isn't there.'

'Is this somehow connected to being non-binary?' I ask.

'No. Gender and sexual orientation are quite separate. I just . . .' she rubs her eyes.

'Sorry, I should know that, yeah.' *God, I'm an idiot.* I try again. 'Thanks for trusting me with this. I think you're amazing, Shell, whatever you are or aren't. And your psych is right. Love and connection takes lots of different forms, it's not all about sex.'

She smiles at me.

'Is there some way I can support you?' I add.

'You could stop asking me about crushing on people, especially Greta. I just like *her*, you know. She's different and seems less complicated than most other people.'

'Well, that's a relief. I'd hate your first partner to be a murderer!' I joke.

She laughs a little. Smiling, we go back to our search.

There's a small desk set a little apart from the painting space. On it is a fancy camera, some academic books, and a laptop with a university sticker on it. It must be Tobias's.

'Hey, check it out. Why is Tobias's laptop here?' I ask.

'No idea,' says Shell. 'He took it from his cabin when they sealed it up, so maybe he's been staying in here?'

His laptop springs to life when I open it. When it asks for a password, I remember the basic password he used for his phone before. I plug that in and boom, it works! What are the chances? Shell laughs a little. I'm smiling smugly to myself when I notice something unnerving. Among the files on the desktop is a folder titled 'Angus Green'.

Why would Tobias have a folder on me?

I move the trackpad to the folder and take a breath. Shell warned me that he knew more than he was letting on . . .

I click into the folder. There's an untitled document and a few photos. One is of me, from media reports over the last year. The other is the same photo of Jane that I found in our kitchen cupboard.

I open the document. All that's on the page is a link. Clicking through, the browser opens up to an anonymous user profile on the website that led me here! There's even the email I was sent.

Shell gasps. I feel like the air has been knocked out of me. All year I've been wondering who was behind that website. How could it have been Tobias all along, someone I hadn't even met until three days ago?

'I can't believe it . . . what does Tobias have to do with me or Jane?'

'I don't know. You keep looking there to see what else you can find, and I'll try the bedroom,' says Shell, disappearing.

I keep opening files but can't find anything else that relates to me.

'Anything there?' I call out.

Shell doesn't reply.

There's nothing out of the ordinary here. 'Found anything in there?' I call out to her.

Still no answer.

I suddenly feel worried. I leave the laptop and head into the bedroom.

Shell is staring at the wall at the end of the room, dumbfounded. I follow her gaze. Covering half the wall are photos of me and newspaper cuttings from the media coverage of the case from last year, as well as clippings from the original case in 2005.

I don't know what to think. All I know is I can't breathe.

'It's like a serial killer's basement,' she whispers. She reaches out to take my hand.

Then the questions start flowing out of my mouth like lava. 'Who even is this John guy? This wall . . . he's like a stalker or something!'

'I don't know. He could be a journalist following the case?' Shell sounds unconvinced.

On the floor there's a folder with more newspaper clippings sticking out. I flick through page after page of media coverage, stopping when I find a few photos I haven't seen before, of me as a baby and toddler. I don't have any photos from back then at all. And these photos were not in the media.

'I've never seen these photos before. Where would a journalist get these?' I say, showing them to Shell.

I really can't breathe. I slump onto the bed and stare at the wall. Shell sits beside me and holds my hand. We sit like this for a moment, not speaking.

'Look, the wall is creepy, but maybe John is close to Jane. That means we are too. You *will* get to meet her! That's got to be a good thing right, after all this time?'

I nod but I don't know what to think, not really.

Shell gets up and opens the wardrobe door. Peering in, she says 'Wait . . . this is women's clothing.'

Suddenly we hear a weird scratching a noise coming from outside. 'What was that?' Shell whispers.

I shake my head. 'Let's get out of here.' I take my phone out of my pocket and snap some photos of the montage on the wall. I feel like I'm going to have a panic attack. The fishhooks are tangled tight inside of me.

We tiptoe to the front door, which Shell has left the key in, as quickly as we can.

As I walk past the window, I notice an alarm clock sitting on the sill. It's round face looks oddly familiar. Then it hits me. Of course. I know who burnt the houseboat. It's been staring us in the face the whole time!

Shell pulls the front door open and I literally bump into her when she stops halfway through the door.

Tobias is standing on the other side of the doorway, holding a knife.

Chapter 37

Fire

He moves forward, with the knife raised. Shell and I both step backwards into the cabin. I can't breathe.

'How did you get in here?' he asks sternly.

Suddenly Kane comes from behind him through the doorway. 'Leave them alone!' he yells, launching himself at him and footy tackling Tobias to the floor. I kick the knife away from his hands and it slides across the floor where Shell swiftly stomps on it with her combat boot.

'What the—' Tobias seems to have no idea what's going on. Kane has him pinned to the floor, holding his hands behind his back.

The wind slams the door closed behind us.

Tobias catches his breath and struggles against Kane. 'Let go, you idiot!'

He catches sight of the pearl-handled knife under Shell's boot and seems to realise what we must have been thinking. He stops struggling and raises his hands in surrender. Kane eases off but doesn't let go.

'Sorry. This is the cake knife we used the other night. Cath said it's from here so I was just returning it.'

We both visibly relax. *For a moment there I thought . . .*

'Oh, my bad,' says Kane sheepishly, letting go of his arms. 'I was coming to help you guys out and I saw Tobias with the knife and . . .'

Tobias gets to his feet and dusts himself off, giving Kane the dirtiest of looks. 'Thug,' he mutters.

Kane glares right back. 'You came at them with a knife, what was I meant to think?'

Regaining his dignity, Tobias looks to me and Shell. 'I did not mean to scare you. But how did you get in here?'

'I borrowed the key from Cath,' replies Shell innocently.

'Oh, did you?' he says mockingly, eyebrow raised.

'We found your laptop,' I say, pointing to the table.

He looks at the table. 'That would make sense, given that I have set myself up in here while my cabin is still a crime scene.'

'Okay, but it doesn't make sense that there's a file about me on your desktop, a link to the website that started all of this, and an anonymous account that emailed me about The Circle, does it?' I ask.

He's clearly furious, his cheeks bulging as he shouts. 'How dare—'

I don't let him finish. 'What about the psycho stalker wall in the bedroom? How is John connected to Jane? I knew you were all lying to me, but this is cruel!' I can barely get the words out, I'm so angry.

Tobias holds his hands up. 'Let me explain.'

'And another thing, I figured out how the boat was burnt now. I know who did it, and how.'

'Who?' Tobias and Shell ask at the same time.

I suddenly shiver as I get that creepy sensation of being watched. Through the window, I can just make out a figure standing outside. They're wearing a black hoodie that hides their face, like a character in a horror film. They have one of those black jackets on, covering their body. I can't tell who it is, but the window is open. They must have heard what I said.

Suddenly they disappear, almost as if I'd imagined them.

Tobias goes to sit down. 'Okay. Tell me what you think you've worked out and we'll take it from there.'

'I more than "think" it, I know it,' I reply.

'C'mon, tell us who did it!' Kane says.

Suddenly Shell interrupts. 'Wait, can you smell smoke?'

I can. We look around in a panic, realising all at once that there's smoke seeping through the side wall of the cabin. A lot of smoke. Within seconds, all four of us are coughing and spluttering.

'What's happening?' Shell panics. The side wall is warping and buckling in the heat. There's a sudden whoosh sound and the curtains on the side window are suddenly on fire, flailing toward us like red tongues. The room is filling with smoke.

That's when I notice that the hooded figure is still outside – watching, waiting.

'Who is that?' I ask, pointing.

'Dunno,' says Shell. 'But we gotta get out of here before it all goes up.'

We rush to the front door, but it's stuck. My eyes and throat are burning from the smoke.

Tobias points to the kitchen. 'Use one of those chairs to break the door. I just have to get something.' He bolts into the bedroom.

Kane picks up a chair and throws it at the front door. It cracks but doesn't shatter all the way. He throws it again and this time the glass showers into pieces. The sudden rush of cool air from outside is a relief, but it makes the flames *whoosh* with intensity. Picking up one of the broken chair legs, Kane punches the remaining glass away from the frame.

Before I have time to react, Shell grabs some towels from the bathroom and runs them under the cold tap.

'Take these!' she yells, flinging a towel to me and Kane. I wrap it around my head and shoulders, like she is doing. 'Now *run*!' she gasps, pushing me and Kane toward the door.

'Tobias, you too!' She flings him a wet towel as he comes back out of the room, holding that big folder we found earlier. He catches the towel awkwardly but gets it up over his head with one hand, using his other hand to grab his laptop from the desk and tuck it under his arm with the folder.

We stumble out of the cabin and start sprinting. Taking a backwards glance at the flames, I spot Hoodie coming toward us.

Shell collapses next to me, and Kane and Tobias both do the same on the other side. We all get back on our feet and start sprinting.

'Help! Fire!' Shell yells as she runs. *Where is everyone?*

I'm looking around wildly in desperation when a glow further up the hill catches my eye. The stone circle is on fire too! What the hell is going on? How can stones burn?

Kane is outrunning us easily, and Shell and Tobias aren't far behind him. Hoodie is gaining on me. I'm too fat and slow to outrun them. I feel faint, like the world is swirling around me, taking me away. The ground disappears and I fall. When I scramble back up it's too late. I'm caught.

The others keep running up to the circle, not realising I've fallen over.

Suddenly Hoodie is right here. They lean over me and pull back their hood. 'Gus.'

'Nash? You?' I say in shock, then black out.

* * *

I wake up with Kane standing over me, saying something I can't hear. 'What happened?' I mumble.

Kane looks relieved. 'You fainted, Goose. I think you breathed in too much smoke.'

I try to sit up but I feel dizzy.

Nash is standing off to the side. Why aren't the others trying to get away from him? He's capable of anything. And all this time I was the one defending him, like an idiot. I really thought I'd solved this case, but I was wrong.

'You tried to kill us!' I whisper hoarsely, pointing at him.

'What?' he says.

'I just saw you behind the cabin!'

'That wasn't . . . I didn't light it. I was watching the fire . . . all that power . . .' he says, eyes wide. He shakes his head, snapping himself back into reality.

'Then why did you chase us?'

'Are you blind?' he yells, pointing to the stone circle. 'I was trying to get help!'

I look at where he is pointing. The stones are on fire, big clouds of smoke billowing from the centre. Then I realise that there is someone else there, standing in the circle, partially hidden from view by the smoke and flames. They seem to be in a black jacket too.

'Come on!' Nash yells and starts running to the circle.

Tobias and Kane help me up and we catch up with Nash. 'We have to stop her,' he yells.

The smoke clears a little and I can see them in the middle of the circle, standing with arms wide, with what looks like the copies of the sale contract in either hand.

A gush of wind makes the smoke clear properly.

It's Greta.

Chapter 38

Clock

'*Stay away!*' Greta yells.

She is standing on the keystone, right in the middle of the circle. The grass around the base of the stones is burning. She has the jerry can of petrol by her feet and a lighter in her hand. The smoke swirls then settles with the wind. I can see her more clearly now. She looks mad, like complete breakdown mad. And she looks way older than nineteen. It's like the whole ordeal has aged her.

She's muttering to herself, moving from one stone to the next, touching them, as if trying to receive a message. She pulls her hand away each time. I'm not sure if she can feel the heat from the fire spreading or just wants to believe there is power running through them into her.

Shell runs over to the circle and puts out her arm to stop us going forward. 'Let me try to speak to her,' she says.

I look behind me. If the fire at cabin four takes hold, it could burn half the cabins, with this fire here burning the rest. Not to mention the bushland surrounding the whole area. While the ground around us is still damp, the grass around the stones must have dried enough to burn with petrol added.

'Are you channelling the power of the stones?' Shell speaks gently as she moves around the circle to look Greta in the eye, one slow step at a time.

Greta looks up, pointing her lighter at Shell like it's a gun.

'No.'

'Then what do you want from them?'

'Fire is pure,' she says, smiling to herself. 'It burns away sins.'

'Was your sin setting the houseboat on fire?' I ask. Shell's head whips over to me in surprise.

Greta gnashes her teeth. 'I only wanted to scare him. I didn't know he'd go to the boat that night.'

Shell composes herself and takes a step closer, just outside the circle now, too close to the flames for my liking. 'You did it to protect your home.'

Greta nods. 'Yes.'

Tobias comes up to stand next to Shell. 'And protect Cath from him.'

'Yes!' she says, louder this time.

'But you were with me when it happened,' says Shell. 'How did you set fire to the boat?'

Greta smiles a creepy little smile.

'You made the gizmo Tobias found,' I say. 'And you used part of Maxine's clock so that it worked as a timer, didn't you?'

She nods her head enthusiastically, almost pleased I've figured it out.

I turn to the others. Tobias lets out a sigh next to me, a resigned look on his face.

'I thought the round part of the device looked familiar, but I couldn't place it until I saw a similar clock in cabin four.'

'Yes,' Greta says gleefully. 'No one would know it was me. I just had to tell you all that Nash was a pyro and you'd all blame him.'

Nash doesn't respond to this. He's just staring at the fire, like someone in love.

'So, you planned it all?' asks Shell. 'You just spent time with me to be your witness?'

'I'm not as stupid as you all think,' Greta snarls, her face breaking out in an unnerving, almost smug grin.

Shell turns her back on Greta and walks away.

'Where are you going?' I yell after her. Now is not the time to sulk. I want to go after her, but we have to stop Greta.

As I look back down the hill, I can see that Sutton and Couttas have found fire extinguishers and are trying to tame the blaze at cabin four. Cath is with them with another fire extinguisher, fighting the fire alongside them.

Kane turns to me. 'I'm going to help,' he says, running to the garage. He darts out a few seconds later holding another fire extinguisher, then heads to cabin four.

Looking past him, I see another car parked by cabin one, a small blue hatchback. There's a woman in an orange coat running from the car to the cabin, but I can't see her clearly. *Who is that?*

I need to focus on Greta. 'I don't think you're stupid,' I say gently. Out the corner of my eye I can see Tobias moving to stand between two of the stones.

'I followed you to cabin four. I heard you say you figured it out, and I could tell you were staring at the clock on the windowsill,' she moans. 'That's when I knew you knew. I had to burn the cabin to keep you away.'

I shudder but nod. 'I get it now.'

'He drove off to town. Why was he on the boat?' Greta says, almost to herself. 'I didn't know . . . he'd be . . . there,' she says, gasping. It turns into a wail.

Cath appears next to Tobias, panting. 'It's okay Greta, you were just trying to scare him,' she says soothingly.

'Traitor!' Greta yells, brandishing the contracts again. Cath steps back as if she's been hit. 'You were gonna sell our home! Traitor!'

'How did you know?' Cath asks, horrified.

'I saw Nash take an envelope from your room the other day. I searched his room and found them!'

Cath puts her hands together in a pleading gesture. 'Nash is so unhappy here, Greta. I agreed to sell, but in the end I couldn't do it to you all. I am going to rescind the contract!' She's got one eye on Greta and another on the flames, trying to see a way through. 'Greta please, come away from the fire.'

Greta picks up the can of petrol and starts to splash more around, fuelling the flames. There's an awful roaring noise as the fire inhales the fuel. Greta throws the contracts on the blaze. The flames claw higher up the stones, the swirling smoke making Greta blur in and out of focus like an apparition.

What do we do? How do we stop her? It won't be long until the fire reaches Greta properly.

Suddenly there's a loud revving noise to the right. Shell comes screeching out of the garage door on the quad bike. She has one of the fire extinguishers in her hand, and another strapped to the back of the bike. Mud flying, she brakes just in time to avoid the stones, then she stands up on the bike and blasts the flames with the extinguisher. Foam flies out everywhere, drenching the flames around the stones, one by one.

She's like some kind of foam-generating superhero.

'This is for making me your alibi, bitch!' Shell yells as she fires the rest of the extinguisher foam at Greta, who drops the petrol and the lighter to cover her eyes.

'Grab her!' shouts Shell. Tobias and Cath run in and pull Greta off the keystone and right out of the circle. Greta stumbles after them, drenched in foam but free of the fire. There's a flash of orange as the woman I saw near cabin four dashes past me. She kneels by Greta, wrapping her coat around her.

'We all make mistakes Greta,' she says softly. Greta starts to wail in her arms and the woman pats her head, smoothing her hair. Then she looks directly up at me.

Now that I can see her face properly for the first time, I don't believe my eyes. It's Jane.

I don't know what to think, what to feel. With the world on fire around me, it's a lot to take in. I look at her, focusing on those sad eyes I know so well. She looks the same, just a bit older, a bit more worn out.

A lifetime of feelings are colliding in my head. The fishhooks are everywhere. I feel my legs starting to wobble beneath me.

Tobias takes over watching Greta, his head swivelling between her crumpled form and the fire. Tentatively, Jane gets up and comes toward me. There's like a hundred expressions moving across her face, just like there's a hundred thoughts flying around in my head.

'Are you okay?' Her voice is controlled, but her eyes are full of tears.

I'm standing there, frozen. I don't know what to say, what to do. She's standing right in front of me now, close enough to touch her.

'Can I hug you?' she asks.

All the conflicted feelings fall away and I just open my arms and let her hug me. She holds me so tight, it's like she's making up for every hug over the years that she never got to give.

It takes a long time before either of us pull away.

Chapter 39

Detective

Back down the hill, it looks like Sutton and Couttas and Kane have put out the fire at cabin four. One side of the building is blackened and steaming, but it doesn't look like there's massive damage, despite the thick smoke snaking up into the sky.

Cath is leading Greta down the hill to the police, arm protectively around her. Greta looks hunched and defeated, like an old woman.

Jane is standing next to me, holding my hand, looking sadly at her blackened cabin. 'Poor Greta. She's not a bad person,' she says quietly. 'But why did she have to burn my place? She knows I'm her friend.'

'*Your* place? Hang on, *you're* John?' I ask.

Jane nods sheepishly. 'Yes. I'll explain everything properly, I promise.' I can't believe the connection between John and Jane is this simple.

'The fire is my fault,' I say. 'We snuck into your cabin and Greta heard me say that I figured out who burnt the houseboat.'

'Ah, I see.'

I feel guilty about the fire, but I'm still pissed off. I hope her unsettling paintings and her creepy wall of photos are gone.

But then I look at her again and that anger fades, like a photo left out in the sun.

We're both not really sure what to say or do. This reunion has been a long time coming and something she must have thought about for many years. It's certainly all I've thought about since I found out about her. And I have so many questions fighting to be at the front of the queue in my head. For now, I don't have the energy for all of this. All I can think about is that she's here, right next to me, like I wanted all this time.

Shell and Kane are standing nearby, watching me and Jane. They look happy for me, but also a bit concerned I think, not sure what to make of her. They are the *best* friends. I think of Kane smashing the door down so we could escape, and fighting the cabin fire. Shell riding like a warrior queen on the quad bike. I'm so lucky to have had their help during this messed-up time.

Tobias looks at us both standing here and sizes things up pretty quickly. 'Shall we ask the police if it is safe to go in and see what we can save?' he asks Jane.

She nods and looks at me nervously. 'We have a lot to talk about, but I want to give you time to catch your breath. And I need to go and see what's left of my life, if that's okay?'

'Sure,' I say.

I'm so not okay yet. With breathing in all that smoke and the feelings swirling around inside of me, catching my breath is exactly what I need to do. For like a week.

As we head back down the hill, I notice a police four-wheel drive and an ambulance parked near Cath's cabin. This must be the detective arriving on the scene, just *after* the nick of time.

Sutton and Couttas come out to greet him. He's an older man in a navy suit. Probably in his late fifties, he has a weatherbeaten face, kind eyes and an impressive goatee.

There is a solemn looking discussion and then lots of pointing, to the houseboat, Tobias's cabin, Jane's cabin, and the stone circle. I can only imagine what the conversation is about. Sutton and Couttas were sent here to secure one crime scene. Now there's like four crime scenes!

He comes over to all of us and introduces himself. 'Detective Guy Carland.' He smells of cheap, overpowering aftershave, and I think I can see crumbs in his goatee, like he's been eating chips.

Behind him, Couttas takes a pair of handcuffs from his belt and cuffs Greta's hands behind her back. Greta looks horrified under the ash covering her face. Couttas takes her arm and starts leading her toward us. 'I didn't mean it to be like this . . . I didn't mean it to be like this . . . I'm sorry . . . I'm sorry,' she mumbles as she passes, her voice barely audible. She sounds so small and broken.

I believe her when she says that she didn't know Walker would be there. But she made choices about burning the boat, Jane's cabin and the stone circle.

'Get me up to speed, Sutton,' Carland says. Sutton starts referring to her notes and pulling evidence bags from her pocket. Couttas walks Greta up to her cabin and follows her inside. Her head is down, not making eye contact with any of us as she goes. He must be keeping guard there, until the detective gets caught up with everything and can interview her formally.

Nash still seems a bit stunned by seeing fire, just like with the houseboat. I wave my hand in front of his face and he snaps back into reality.

Suddenly I hear an AC/DC horn riff from the road. 'Wait, isn't that your awful car horn?' Shell says to Kane.

He grins. 'Mum's got the same one. She's just rocked up with both your mums.'

Fiona Parker's red Toyota RAV 4 has pulled up outside the entrance to the community. Fiona gets out of the driver's seat, wearing her usual fitness gear, but covered with a silver puffer jacket. She leaps across the muddy ground in her fancy trainers.

Out of the back seat stumbles Cheryl Oliver, Shell's mum. She's big and tall with a hugely elaborate blonde hairdo. She is wearing a fancy pink pants suit with massive high heels. She has to unfold herself to get out, like a large, rich spider. Her heels sink straight into the mud.

Meg, my mum, steps out of the passenger seat, walking gingerly in the wet ground, trying not to put too much pressure on her legs. She is small and thin and wearing a plain black top over wide leg jeans and looks like a doll compared to Cheryl.

Are these the most unlikely three friends in the world? I look back at Cath and Maxine standing at Greta's door. Huh. Maybe not.

'How can your mum walk in those heels?' I ask Shell.

'She can swim and ski in them too,' she replies drolly.

'Gussy,' Mum yells. She starts to make her way toward me, carefully stepping over the worst of the mud. She throws her arms around me and it is strange to suddenly compare motherly hugs and their perfumes. The floral perfume with a hint of bleach that Mum usually smells of feels very reassuring today.

She holds up a shapeless lump of purple knitting. 'It's a cap for you,' she says, and puts it on my big square head. I look at my reflection on my phone. It looks awful and wonky, but I smile, pleased to see her.

Cheryl is kissing Shell and telling her she needs a good wash and that they will go to a spa when this is all over. Shell seems less horrified by her mother than usual. Cheryl's face and hair seem to envelop Shell and she disappears into her mother's big arms. I can just make out a muffled, 'Relax Cheryl, I'm totally fine.' But she leans into her embrace, clearly glad she's here.

Fiona comes over and gives Kane a big hug. This is unusual for them, not something I've really seen them do before. Maybe she really has been worried about him and all the sleepwalking. Her ponytail bounces all over the place as she nods, listening to whatever he's telling her. She's wearing a bright yellow T-shirt under her silver jacket that says, 'Everything you want is on the other side of fear'.

'Tell me everything,' Mum says, 'Don't leave out a thing. Oh, did that cabin just catch fire today?' She points to Jane's cabin, just as Jane walks out of the door, carrying a couple of rescued paintings under one arm and that big camera I saw earlier. She looks over to me and then to Mum awkwardly.

The colour drains from Mum's face. 'She's here after all? You found her.'

She squints back at Jane. Her hand grips mine more tightly than before. It feels almost possessive.

'Yes,' I reply with a weird combination of joy and sadness and exhaustion. 'I found her.'

Chapter 40

Noodles

We're sitting in Maxine's cabin, which is a nice change. Mum, who likes a clinically tidy house, is a bit thrown by the sheer volume of animal print everywhere. She sits on the couch, frowning at a lion shaped cushion and grimacing at the garish pink leopard skin rug beneath her feet, as if it will rear up and bite her.

'It's like an ugly zoo exploded in here,' she whispers to me.

Sitting here with Mum, Tobias and Jane feels like I've been summoned to see the principal at school, but worse. Like seeing my psych when I know I'm going to face some dark stuff that will hurt.

The room is deathly quiet. Jane clears her throat several times and rubs her hands together. I try to compare them to my own, looking for similarities. I find myself staring at her a lot. I seem to have her eyes, maybe. And there's a hint of my funny square-shaped face, but just a hint.

She gets up and starts faffing about in the kitchen, opening cupboard doors. 'Do you still like two-minute noodles?' she asks, tentatively. 'I think Maxine has some here.'

'Yes, he does,' says Mum, bristling a little. You could cut the tension between them with a knife. Jane throws her a look.

Tobias pats the couch next to him. 'Come and sit down, Jane. That can wait.'

This is a world of weird right now.

When I was a kid, I used to be amazed by Doctor Who's TARDIS and how it was bigger on the inside than the outside. I always felt the other way round. To cope, I used to crawl into my cubbyhouse and try to make myself even smaller. Later, I added cutting to my cubbyhouse visits.

Right now, faced with all of this, I wish that blue box would appear and whisk me away.

Reluctantly Jane shuts the cupboard door and walks back to the couch. There's something about the two of them, Tobias and Jane, sitting next to each other. They look like parents about to tell their kid off.

Jane puts her hands together. Her fingers are thin and the nails look bitten. There are flecks of paint dried into her knuckles.

'I know this must be strange for you, after all these years,' she says. 'And I know you have questions. And you may be angry. Let's just go at your pace.'

Where do I begin? There's so many files open in my brain that it'll probably completely crash.

I'm trying to decide where to start, when suddenly I'm hit by a wave of anger.

'Why haven't you contacted me before now?'

She looks surprised, blinking.

I keep going. 'I really thought once my case was all over the news that you would contact me. And when you didn't, I thought you either didn't want to know or you were dead. Neither was good.'

Jane audibly gulps. Maybe she wasn't prepared to be verbally slapped in the face like that. Not right up front at least. Even Mum seems a bit surprised. Has Jane played this out in her head a million times over the years like I have? Was it snarky like this, or all friendly and nice, I wonder?

Jane collects herself and looks me in the eye. 'I wasn't in a good place. I had a bit of a breakdown a few years back, and honestly I'm still a bit fragile these days. That's why I'm here. When I saw the media coverage, I was thrilled. But also terrified. No matter how much I wanted to see you, I knew you would blame me for what happened.'

'I blame you for neglecting me.' I've only ever told Dr Yamada this. The words come out of my mouth as a full accusation.

She nods her head. 'I accept that. I was a bad mother.'

'Yes, you were,' snaps Mum, who I can feel shifting impatiently on the couch next to me.

Tobias nudges Jane gently. 'Keep going with your story. We can save the assignation of blame for another time.'

Jane nods. 'I put off contacting you for a while. Then a while longer. I started to feel a bit better, but I worried about how'd you react when I did contact you. You had already been through enough, and you had another mum who clearly loves you, and a life of your own, and I didn't want to blow that all up. I asked Tobias to send you that message.'

Mum nods at the indirect acknowledgment from Jane.

'But why hide once I was here?' I ask. 'Why not just say who you were? Why all these stupid games?' The whole thing is super frustrating. My cuts are itching.

She rubs her face nervously. 'I was scared. I wanted Tobias to meet you first and gauge just *how* angry you were with me. I begged everyone to pretend they didn't know who I was. They only agreed because they knew I wanted to meet you on my own terms. This community has been so good to me, so supportive. I was going to come to Cath's party to meet you but . . . the storm hit.'

She starts picking at a speck of paint on one of her fingernails. 'I couldn't get through on the phone and the flooding stopped me from coming home, so I was stuck in Walliss and had to stay the night.

And then when I was finally able to talk to Tobias, I heard about Walker. I was terrified that I had put you in danger all over again.'

Tobias smiles at Jane. 'I was keeping an eye on him for you.'

Mum shifts in her seat, asserting herself. 'A lot has happened to Gus in the last year. A hell of a lot. I think you owe Gus a full explanation, right from the start.'

Jane nods. 'You're right, I do,' she stares up at me, quite intently. 'I see a whole other life in your eyes.'

I feel the heat rising up my neck. 'Well yeah, I had a life. And then I found out I was living the wrong one.'

She shudders and Tobias puts his arm around her shoulders. She sighs, 'When I think of everything that happened to you . . .' her voice drifts off. She is starting to tear up.

Mum runs her hands through my messy hair. 'You doing okay? You want to go on?'

I nod and turn back to Jane. 'Did you get married or have other kids?'

A tear seeps out her eye. 'No. After everything that happened, it took a few years to piece myself back together. I'm still not sure that I am together, but I'm getting there.'

She grabs Tobias's hand and he smiles at her.

'Wait, are you two a couple?' I ask. Seriously, could this situation get any nuttier? Maybe the lamp and the rug are dating too.

Tobias blushes. 'We are spending time together, yes.'

'Is this the "secret" Walker had over you?' I ask.

'I believe so. Not very shocking I am afraid,' he laughs.

I don't know why, but I'm suddenly furious at Tobias. 'You knew where she was the entire time, and you knew how desperate I was to find her, but you said nothing? That's a shitty thing to do.' I instinctively walk over to the fridge, ready to inhale anything that's in there. Mum follows, limping.

'Okay, maybe let's take a breath,' she says. She eyes one of the paintings leaning against the wall that were rescued from Jane's cabin. 'You have an, um, interesting style.'

Jane's eyes flash a little. 'Do you know much about art?'

'Nothing, I don't have an artistic bone in my body,' she smiles. 'How do you make it look like it's changing colour?'

She sees it too!

Jane brightens up at the question. 'I use normal oils, but mix in a particular type of paint that has a pearl flake through it that's actually used for cars. The paint changes colour depending on the light source and the angle you look at it.'

Now I get it. 'Wow. That's clever. The changing colour really threw me.'

Tobias stands up too and smiles at Mum. 'Why don't you and your friends stay to see the southern lights? They are happening tonight after sunset. They are a spectacular, once-in-a-decade event by all accounts.'

Now Jane is standing too. 'Please do. After all this time, I don't think I could bear you just leaving now. We don't have to talk about the past if you don't want. Or we can. It's up to you.'

I can see real fear in her eyes. Or need. Maybe both.

I look at Mum, who nods. I take a deep breath. 'We'll stay and see the lights.'

Jane nods enthusiastically, gratefully taking this crumb from me. 'I'm going to be taking lots of photos tonight for reference for painting, once I get some more supplies. You can help me if you want?'

That needy look cracks my heart a little. And with that cracking, I realise that I *do* want to know her and I *do* want to help her take photos. I smile at her, but I look at Mum out the corner of my eye. *What is she thinking?*

Chapter 41

Earring

Two hours later, we're all back in Cath's cabin. *Again.*

Detective Carland coughs before addressing us all. He has his hands behind his back like he is addressing a lecture hall full of students. His goatee bristles as he talks.

'We've now completed basic investigations. As some of you may know, we have heard a full confession from young Greta.'

Cath sighs and Maxine shudders.

'Once the homicide and arson teams get here from Melbourne, we will be able to conduct a proper investigation and take care of the deceased.'

'What will happen to Greta?' Cath asks.

He turns to her. 'We've only started to investigate this case, but she'll likely be charged with manslaughter. There seems to be no evidence of intent to kill. The maximum for manslaughter in Victoria is a twenty-five-year custodial sentence. But given that she has now confessed, she'll likely get a lesser sentence. Though there's the other fires that endangered lives to consider.'

Cath shakes her head and puts her hand on Maxine's shoulder.

'Prison! She's so young,' Cath says.

Sutton turns to me and Shell and Kane. 'You kids are lucky things worked out okay. You shouldn't go interfering in police business,' her face softens, just slightly. 'But well done for figuring it all out and stopping the whole area from going up in flames. You will make a good police officer one day, Gus.' Her eyes flick over to Kane. 'And you might consider a future in firefighting, after the way you sprang into action to help Couttas and me.'

I smile. Kane's face lights up.

Shell clears her throat. 'Senior Constable Sutton, do you still have that metal thing you found on the houseboat?'

Sutton nods.

'Can I show it to someone?'

'Why not,' she says, handing over the evidence bag. Shell takes it and passes it to Maxine. 'Is this your missing earring?'

Maxine's shoulders slump. 'Yes. I knew I lost it on the houseboat when I was looking for something. I didn't want it being found by someone else' – she eyes Cath warily – 'so I went back for it when I thought Walker wouldn't be there.'

'What were you looking for?' Shell asks.

Maxine sighs. 'Money. I knew he kept cash in a drawer on the houseboat, but it was locked and I couldn't open it. I tried to use my earring to jimmy it open but it didn't work. I must have dropped it when I left.'

Cath looks up in surprise. 'How did you know he kept money there?'

Maxine looks at her knowingly. She seems to go to say one thing, then stops and sighs. 'You weren't the only one he liked to spend time with, Cath.'

Both women stare at one another for a moment. Maxine looks away first. 'I told Simon all about my past, more fool me. I need money because my ex has taken my daughter and moved interstate and not told me where they are. I need to pay someone to help me track them down. But Simon wouldn't lend me any. He was just using me, hoping I'd help get Cath to sell.'

Maxine's eyes dart over to the other side of the room, where Carland and Sutton are talking, going over notes. Furtively, she produces Walker's watch from her pocket and gently places it on the coffee table. 'I'm ashamed to say that I took this from Simon while he was in cabin five. I just need to see my daughter again.'

I'm surprised she's admitting this in front of the police, even if they're not paying attention.

'How did we not find it?' I say.

'It was hidden inside the freezer. If it can survive a rocket explosion, it can survive inside a tub of ice cream,' she replies with a wry smile.

Wow, the revelations are coming thick and fast now. Shell and Kane and I are eating it all up.

Carland and Sutton turn their attention back to us. Sutton closes her notebook. 'We're going to head off for tonight and take Greta into custody. We'll be back in the morning to meet the other teams when they arrive. You kids may have solved this crime, but there's still a lot of work to do for us here. Leave this to us now, *please.*'

She tips her hat at me as they leave, ignoring the watch completely, as if she never saw it.

Chapter 42

Lights

Later that day, as the sun fades away, we are all outside having a drink under Cath's now very crowded verandah. Some of us are on chairs, some are leaning against the poles holding the verandah up, some are just standing around.

It's super strange to see our mums here, after days of just the community. There's so much energy, after the draining, stormy, confusing time we've all had.

Cath stands off to one side, watching everyone. She seems too exhausted to talk. She looks lost without Greta.

We're in that strange lull after the storm. The last few days have been a rollercoaster of tension, so despite everything, there's this sense of relief. Everyone is talking a bit more than they had been, mainly to Jane, filling her in on what happened while she was gone. She seems a bit overwhelmed by all the information coming at her, as well as the pressure of us meeting, I guess. I feel the same.

Mum smiles at me. 'You just can't stay out of trouble, can you?' She ruffles my stupid hair. Jane watches us. I wonder if she is jealous of Mum. Does she suddenly want to step in and assert her motherhood with me? Or is just being here a big enough ordeal for her?

Me and Mum and Shell and Kane and their mums are all going to stay in a hotel in Walliss tonight. It's been a strange few days and I'm looking forward to getting out of here. I'm tired of Shell's snoring and the general lack of privacy. Plus I really want a long hot shower.

There's a loud hoot of laughter and I look over to see Cheryl, towering over everyone, holding a bottle of white wine, presumably left over from the fiftieth. She's a big woman with big hair and a big heart. It's hard not to smile at her antics.

Maxine and Mum and Fiona hold up their glasses to Cheryl and she gives them a generous pour. Jane covers her glass and shakes her head. 'Thanks, but I don't drink.' Looking at me pointedly, she adds, 'Sober for five-and-a-half years now.'

Maxine lowers her glass wistfully before pouring her drink on the ground. 'I think it's time I followed suit.'

'Well done you. I couldn't survive without wine time and the odd happy pill,' laughs Cheryl.

Shell shakes her head. 'You are so cringe, Cheryl. Someone has died and their killer tried to burn themselves and us. It's not a time for a party.' Shell is looking at her mother with a combination of love and annoyance, which is literally their whole relationship.

Her mother rolls her eyes at her, in the exact same way that Shell does to me. 'You lot are alive, that's reason enough for a party in my books.'

Fiona nods her agreement. 'I hope this terrible experience hasn't made your sleepwalking any worse, Kane.'

Kane looks at her in horror. 'Don't tell everyone!'

Fiona tuts at him. 'There's nothing to be ashamed about. It's just a medical issue, like your knee last year. We'll soon get to the bottom of it.'

I give Kane a look. He nods resignedly and quietly says to her, 'I think I've figured it out. We can talk about it later, okay?'

'That's great news,' she says, giving him a gentle kiss on the cheek that he backs away from. She just laughs and takes another swig of wine.

Nash is looking less surly than usual. He actually appears to be smiling. I guess it's more like a cross between a smile and a scowl, but still that's progress.

'Why are you smiling?' I ask, staring back at him.

He breaks out into a big grin. 'We all had you fooled with the Jane and John routine, didn't we,' he says smugly.

'Yeah, nice one. It was really upsetting, not knowing what was going on.'

His face drops a little. 'It was meant to end once Jane arrived.'

'But she didn't, and you lot kept up the lies anyway.'

'I came close to telling you at one point, but it wasn't up to me. I promised Jane and Mum. We all did. She was terrified you'd hate her so she wanted us to see if you did. But I did leave that photo in the cabin for you to find . . .'

Oh. 'That was you?'

He grins at me. It's like he's actually becoming a nice person in front of my eyes. We stare at each other. I feel like he wants to kiss me. I definitely want to kiss him. Our faces get closer. I can feel the warmth of his breath.

Suddenly we're startled apart by Cath clapping her hands loudly. 'Okay everyone, it's all over now. Let's draw a line under it and go and see the southern lights!'

Everyone murmurs their agreement. I look at Nash but he looks away. I think the moment is gone.

We all put on black jackets from Cath's endless supply and walk outside and back up the hill. Jane looks sadly at her burnt cabin as we pass by.

I'd never really heard of the lights until this weekend. I knew about the northern lights obviously, but didn't know we had our own version in Australia.

Jane's taking photos with her serious looking camera with an impressive telephoto lens. I'm glad she was able to rescue it from her cabin.

The rest of us are using our phones or simply watching, like I am. I just want to absorb it.

The night sky is like a multicoloured blanket about us. There are special dots of lights everywhere, and soon they are swamped by this wave of magical colour. Dramatically, the sky goes purple and pinkish, on top of a layer of green. It swims around our heads like it's alive.

It's cool standing here with this strange combination of people. We're all here together under an exploding sky on a hill with a circle of stones older than time. Our faces are illuminated by this stunning, shared, ancient experience. We're looking up to the sky, as if trying to find answers to big questions or trying to find something special inside of ourselves. Like a song no one else can sing.

It makes me feel connected to something far bigger. I feel bigger on the inside, at last.

I look around and see Shell, mesmerised by the lights. Kane is flexing in front of Maxine, who is giggling, filming him on his phone. Cath is smiling at the sky and seems more relaxed now. Tobias is transfixed. Even Nash seems impressed. As if he feels me watching, he turns and smiles at me again.

Mum is standing on one side of me, Jane is on the other side, all three of us drenched in ribbons of green and pink light.

Acknowledgements

Having the first Gus book published was a childhood dream come true for me. And if that had been the total sum of my career as an author, I would have been cool with that. So to have a second Gus book published now is all just icing on the cake. *Is this a series now?*

Major thanks to Wakefield Press for backing me a second time and for Maddy Sexton for commissioning another book and being an amazing and supportive editor and champion. Thanks also to the Wakefield team of Polly Grant Butler and Carney Sims and the sales reps, as well as Josh Durham for another evocative cover design.

Big thanks as always to Jane Novak for being my agent. I am lucky to have you in my corner.

I am indebted to author mates Amy Doak and R.W.R. McDonald for giving me great feedback on this story. Massive thanks to them, and also Holden Sheppard and Kate Emery, for agreeing to grace the cover with your very kind author endorsements.

Thanks again to my expert advisors: Kate Ursprung for medical knowledge, Detective Adam [redacted] for police procedural advice, and some kind people who shared their stories about self-harm and pyromania.

Now to shout out writer mates. One of the best aspects of being published is you get all these amazing authors welcoming you to the 'club' with open arms (a book in one hand and a drink in the other).

Thanks for the advice and friendship and coming to events and generally listening to me drone on: Jono Butler, Matt Ryan Davies, Amy Doak, R.W.R. McDonald, Nilima Rao, Holden Sheppard, plus both the crazy talented 2023 and 2024 Debut Crews. Thanks also to The Prologues: Deb Crabtree, Karen McKnight, Imbi Neeme, Edwina Preston, and Clive Wanbrough.

Another cool thing about being published is you get to meet readers. I am very grateful for all the readers, young and old, who I've met through events, through amazing libraries and librarians (hello Helen Farch), through incredibly supportive booksellers, through writers festivals, through book clubs, through schools, and just by reaching out to me. I've been overwhelmed by the response to Gus and humbled by your kind words.

Sadly, there are many family members gone, but thanks to Bianca Rogers, Peter Rogers, and Kelly White for putting up with me. I wish Ira and Stan Hunter, and Kay Rogers and Guy Stewart were here to see this amazing new chapter in my life continue to unfold.

Last, but never least, thanks to my partner Dean Walliss for always being my first reader and my biggest fan.

Finally, THANK YOU reader for buying or borrowing this book or writing a review or talking about it on a podcast or sharing it on socials. Words can't express how happy that makes me.

Having a tough time and need someone to talk to right now?
The following confidential services are there to
listen and help you out 24/7.

Kids Helpline

1800 551 800

www.kidshelpline.com.au

Headspace

1800 650 890

www.headspace.org.au

Wakefield Press is an independent publishing and
distribution company based in Adelaide, South Australia.
We love good stories and publish beautiful books.
To see our full range of books, please visit our website at
www.wakefieldpress.com.au
where all titles are available for purchase.
To keep up with our latest releases and news,
subscribe to the Wakefield Weekly at
https://mailchi.mp/wakefieldpress/subscribe

Find us!

Facebook: www.facebook.com/wakefield.press
Instagram: www.instagram.com/wakefieldpress